Love is
a time of enchantment:
in it all days are fair and all fields
green. Youth is blest by it,
old age made benign:
the eyes of love see
roses blooming in December,
and sunshine through rain. Verily
is the time of true-love
a time of enchantment — and
Oh! how eager is woman
to be bewitched!

THE AWAKENED HEART

To Hilary, everything seemed to be changing. First Philip, whose brusqueness now they were in Africa came like a blow, and then her sister, Fay, whose marriage was tottering and whose life seemed dark with secrets. Almost unconsciously Hilary changed too, as she left her childishness behind. Her love for Philip, her anxiety for Fay and her acceptance of life in a strange country all helped to awaken her heart and prepare her for both overwhelming terror and overwhelming love.

CLARE BRETON SMITH

◆

THE AWAKENED HEART

Complete and Unabridged

ULVERSCROFT
Leicester

First published in Great Britain in 1959

First Large Print Edition
published September 1992

British Library CIP Data

Smith, Clare Breton
   The awakened heart.—Large print ed.—
Ulverscroft large print series: romance
I. Title
823.914 [F]

ISBN 0–7089–2719–X

Published by
F. A. Thorpe (Publishing) Ltd.
Anstey, Leicestershire
Set by Words & Graphics Ltd.
Anstey, Leicestershire
Printed and bound in Great Britain by
T. J. Press (Padstow) Ltd., Padstow, Cornwall

1

HILARY DALE sat forward eagerly in her seat, gazing out of the window of the plane at the ground far below. At first she had only got glimpses of sun-kissed Africa through rents in the massed clouds but now the clouds had gone and she could see vast stretches of dark earth and an occasional silvery gleam which must be a river.

And then it happened.

One moment, she was feeling safe and happy, almost accustomed to the occasional drop of the plane as they hit an air pocket — and the next moment, she was terrified.

The crowded plane was still noisy, the passengers talking and laughing, but the noise suddenly seemed shrill. It was as if everyone was talking very loudly yet without sense, because they were all waiting and listening for something.

She had read once that an animal scents fear. For the first time she

1

understood. Right down the plane, like the streaking flame of an uncontrollable bush-fire, fear raced.

She turned her head and saw that the pilot was walking down the aisle between the seats. He was fair and chubby-faced but his mouth was a tight line.

As she turned her head Philip Randel, sitting next to her, glanced down at the girl's small, three-cornered face. He had felt the fear at the same moment but he had been prepared. He had been aware that for a considerable time they had been losing height and circling, probably to get rid of surplus fuel. He was also aware that one engine had been faltering and had now packed up.

He looked down at the girl and felt concern. She looked young to be travelling alone. He had noticed her at London Airport for she had been the only person, save for himself, without someone to see her off. A slight girl, she had the look of a waif about her, with that rather odd face, the huge dark eyes and absurdly-curling long black lashes. She was slim, perhaps too thin; she looked almost frail and yet there was an indomitable quality about her.

When he found her sitting by his side in the plane he had been a little vexed, for he was chary of lone females on long journeys; they could be so boring. And so irritating if they decided to hang on. But she had not looked at him, had never opened her mouth. She did not smoke, did not drink, ate her food without complaint and spent most of her time looking out of the window.

So he had relaxed, closing his eyes, worrying at his problem, which, he told himself, was no problem. It was quite simple. Yet he had flown two thousand miles to London and back on a mission that had nothing to do with him, but was merely an excuse to get away, in the hope that he could view his problem more sanely from a distance. But he was just as bewildered, just as vexed with himself, just as torn in two as he had been before he left.

Now he saw the girl's face lose colour, watched the way her small white teeth bit into her lower lip.

"It's all right," he said quietly. "If anything was wrong they would tell us."

3

She turned to stare at him and he watched her strangely luminous dark eyes focus and see him. "I suppose they would," she said uncertainly. She had a pleasant voice, low and slightly husky. She spoke oddly, too, with a little pause before the words came out in a sort of breathless rush.

Hilary went on staring at him without realizing it. She was trying to tell herself that he was right. There was no danger. Inside her, her heart began to thud madly and she felt the palms of her hands grow sticky.

She saw a tall, broad-shouldered, black-haired man with cool grey eyes, a very firm mouth and a big chin. She guessed his age to be about thirty-five. She had noticed him vaguely at the airport. Only vaguely, because she had been so bewildered that she had no time for curiosity. She had wanted to rush home to the security of the quiet village, to the certainty that her mother was there, the dear familiar things. She had hated her isolation, the hollow voices that came thundering over the tannoy, had stared at the huge silver monsters on the tarmac

4

field and had wondered how on earth they would leave the ground. She had sunk into her seat trying not to clench her fists, aware someone was by her side, but too occupied with trying to fasten her seatbelt with hands that would tremble, to notice him. After the first fright when the engines roared so powerfully and the whole plane vibrated — after that bad moment when they ran down the runway and she wondered if the heavy, packed plane would ever rise after that, all had been strangely wonderful and her fear had vanished. In an incredibly short time they had been above the clouds in a sky so blue that it was unbelievable. How thankful she had been to be sitting by the window; she had leaned forward ecstatically, watching. Seeing the cliffs of Dover, so white and stalwart against the grey-green sea — flying high again and content to watch the lovely clouds. There had been so many things to watch and be thrilled by, that she had not even noticed that the tall, distinguished-looking man with a strange air of authority, whom she had noticed at the airport, was her neighbour.

He spoke again, watching her mobile young face with interest. "Is this your first flight?"

"Yes." She twisted her hands, some of her fear returning.

"You look very young to be travelling alone."

She smiled. "I'm twenty."

He lifted dark eyebrows with amusement. "A wonderful age."

"Oh, do you think so?" she said, with the same breathless little rush. "I don't. I think one is terribly unsure at this age."

What a child she looked. Why did girls these days go in for this short elfin haircut? She had dark brown hair, cut very short and with a wispy fringe which seemed to accentuate the size of her dark eyes. He noticed that she wore only a dusting of powder and a pale pink lipstick. It suited her. He noticed, too, that she was very plainly dressed in a grey tweed suit with a white blouse and a little grey beret set squarely on her head. She looked more like a schoolgirl than anything else.

The conversation round them hushed so abruptly that the silence could be felt almost physically. Both turned to look and saw that the pilot was leaning against the door that led to the staff quarters and was smiling. But his smile did not reach his eyes.

"There is no cause for alarm," he said casually. "But we are going to make a forced landing. One of the engines is playing up; there is very bad weather ahead and we think this is the wisest course." He drawled his words, but Hilary saw the way his lazy eyes were looking rapidly down the plane at the waiting passengers. "We have been in touch with the nearest town and they are sending out transport immediately to pick you all up and take you to the airport so that you can continue your journey. Now, would you all please fasten your seat-belts as it may be a bumpy landing." He smiled, and this time, the smile reached his eyes. "I promise you there is no danger. I've made a great many forced landings and never lost a plane yet."

"Nor a passenger?" a fat man joked from one of the front seats.

The pilot looked shocked. "Nor a passenger," he said gravely and vanished through the door behind him, as the pretty blonde hostess moved down the gangway, helping people adjust their seatbelts.

"Can you manage yours?" Philip Randel asked as he watched Hilary fumble clumsily with the fastening of her belt.

"I — I think so." She kept her face bent, feeling her cheeks burn, hoping he would not see the way her hands trembled.

She sat passively as he removed her hands from the clasp and deftly fastened it for her. Then he took hold of her hand and held it tightly.

"It'll be all right," he said gently.

She felt her eyes fill with tears and she blinked fast and furiously. Tears would be the final humiliation. But his voice had been so kind and she was unused to kindness. Her mother believed that you were hurt less if you were brought up to be tough.

"What part of England do you come from?" Philip asked. He was very conscious of the tension in the plane.

"Somerset." She had to force herself

to speak. Every nerve in her body was tense. The nose of the plane seemed to be pointed earthwards at a sharp angle. "Near Bristol." Her throat felt dry and painful. She clung to his hand, without realizing what she was doing.

"I know Bristol. Lovely country round there. So peaceful — so typically English. What are you doing, travelling so far alone?"

She knew he meant to help her. Yet it had the reverse effect. It was sheer torture to marshal her thoughts, to keep her voice normal.

"I am going to stay with my sister in Africa. She is going to have a baby."

What a strange noise the engine was making. Now she could see dark forests on the earth below. Would there be any cleared space big enough for them to land?

"You can be sure the pilot knows what he is doing," Philip said.

She looked at him sharply, sensing a rebuke. "I'm sorry I'm such a coward," she said huskily.

His hand tightened round hers. "You're not. You're being damned brave." He smiled at her. "Don't you know that the bravest people are those who are afraid and yet go on?"

She smiled shakily. "I haven't much choice."

He chuckled. "I didn't think of that."

Now the earth, when she turned to the window, seemed to be very close — she could see great masses of trees with a huge great shadow moving over them like an evil great bird. The plane wheeled so that the earth was now sideways.

"Hang on," Philip said quietly. "There may be a bit of a bump."

She closed her eyes and as the earth came up to meet them, his hand gripped hers. There was an unnatural hush in the plane, and then there was a bump — another bump — another and then the plane seemed to be rolling forward slowly and she opened her eyes and saw that they had landed on a flat sandy piece of ground and that huge masses of trees surrounded them. The plane gave a curious lopsided jolt as it stopped, as if trying to tilt forward on its nose and abruptly the silence was broken everyone was talking and laughing shrilly, somewhere there was the sound of a quickly stifled hysterical sob, a baby began to wail plaintively, two children shouted excitedly.

The hostess came down the plane again, all smiles and looking as pleased as if she had just landed the plane herself, telling them to be patient and that everyone could get out and 'stretch their legs'.

Hilary relaxed and was embarrassed to find she was still clinging very tightly to her neighbour's hand. She let go and moved back in her seat, smiling at him nervously.

"I told you we'd be all right," he said, "but you didn't believe me."

"I . . . I'm sorry I was such a coward."

He smiled. "It was a nasty experience on your first flight. Feel like a walk?"

Just in time she stopped herself from giggling. She was trembling all over.

"It sounds so funny," she said in excuse. "A moment ago, I was waiting to be killed and now you ask me to go for a walk."

"We were all scared," he said. "The pilot most of all, I expect. A breath of fresh air will do us good."

The other passengers had all been pushing and jostling their way out of the plane, as if they could not bear to stay inside any longer. Now Philip and Hilary could walk down the aisle at ease. Philip helped her out of the plane.

The hot air hit them like a blast from a furnace. The sun streamed down, instantly drying and burning the skin. The plane had landed on a flat sandy stretch surrounded on three sides by apparently impenetrable forests. Straight ahead of them, the sand seemed to vanish into the air and they followed the other passengers curiously, walking past the nose of the plane and on through the burning sunshine to where a group of people were standing, staring and exclaiming.

Hilary caught her breath. The flat sandy ground dropped away abruptly to fall down a steep mountainside. It was as if they were on the edge of the world — far, far beneath them lay a valley, shrouded in mist. They could see a glimpse of a silver ribbon winding below — a red thin line that must be a road.

"It's probably three thousand feet down," he said thoughtfully. "I wish I had my binoculars unpacked — we might see some game."

She turned her young eager face towards him. "I'm longing to see giraffes galloping."

She spoke like a child and he was suddenly bored. "Let's go back — looks as if the pilot is giving instructions."

She turned obediently, giving one last breathless look at the sleeping valley. As they walked over the hot sand that burned through the soles of her shoes, she glanced anxiously at the man by her side. He walked with such long effortless strides that she had to almost run to keep up with him. Now he was looking vexed. She wondered if she had said anything to offend him.

They listened to the instructions. No one was to wander away from the plane. The crew would clear a space under the trees to afford shade but no one must leave the clearing. This was wild game country and no lives must be endangered. That was an order. The food and water would be rationed; lighting in the plane would be by lamps and these must be conserved in case they had to spend two nights in the plane. Help would come as soon as it was humanly possible but the rescuing trucks might have to be assisted by a bulldozer before they could reach here. There was no cause for alarm if everyone obeyed orders.

The pilot spoke in a crisp authoritative manner. He spoke, Hilary thought, with the same crispness that her companion used sometimes. She glanced up at him. He was looking bored and a little angry. She wondered what was wrong and if there was anything she could do. Perhaps he had a wife who would worry about this delay.

★ ★ ★

The day dragged by. Unbearably hot — with crying children and fretful babies — and harassed mothers who harassed still more the cheerful little hostess. Philip had gone off to chat with the crew and Hilary, accepting the unintentional rebuff as deserved — how could she have clung to his hand like that? What must he think of her? — helped the hostess as much as she could by amusing the small children, helping to set out the frugal meal.

It was a relief when the sky turned to brilliant crimsons and orange and the sun slowly sank, a great vermilion ball in a wonderful sky as everybody returned to the plane for the night.

Philip was already in his seat and he stood up to let Hilary pass him. Then he arranged the rug they had been given over her knees. He smiled and although she could only just see his face in the dim light, she knew by his voice that he was no longer irritable with her.

"It seems absurd but we can't go on calling one another you — I'm Philip Randel."

"I'm Hilary Dale."

"How do you do?" he said formally and shook her hand.

"Quite well — " she began and then coloured furiously as she remembered how often she had been told the correct answer to that was another: "How do you do." She murmured the words quickly. How stupid it sounded.

Philip chuckled. "Quite a Dr. Livingstone, I presume, touch about it, isn't there?"

She laughed, hoping he would not ask her if she understood what he meant. The night was dark outside. She looked through the window and shivered a little, wondering if huge elephants roamed in the forest; if somewhere out there a lion waited.

In the gloom, most of the passengers were talking. A long night lay ahead and there was no sense in trying to go to sleep too early.

"You said you were coming out to stay with your sister to help her. Do you know anything about babies?" She heard the amusement in his voice but she did not mind — it was kindly amusement, not mocking.

"I don't," she said honestly, "and I'm scared stiff. I've bought masses of books and have read them but I think it'll be very different with a real baby. I just hope I don't do anything silly. It's hard to imagine my sister with a boy of nearly four and another baby on the way. She was always so gay. So — "

It was strange, lying there in the tilted chair and talking quietly to Philip. They enjoyed a strangely intimate isolation for no one paid them any attention and she found it easy to talk to him.

Philip listened, bored but polite, at first, because he was sorry for the girl on her own; but then with interest. It was about a world he had never known. Hilary spoke well, bringing to life the enormous quiet vicarage in the Somersetshire village — the huge rooms, of which all but four were closed up. She spoke of her mother; tall, too thin, once a keen gardener, but suffering from chronic anaemia which caused her to do less and less, so that nowadays she rarely left the sunny warm kitchen. He could see her, loving but undemonstrative, teaching her daughters to be 'tough' and never realising how much her youngest one craved affection. Hilary talked of her father proudly but somehow Philip read between the lines and saw him as he was — a huge, healthy man with no patience for illness, with a great love for mankind and a 'vocation' and little time for his own family. He was a preacher, travelling

17

the length and breadth of the country to spread the 'message'.

"That's why he was given this tiny parish so that he could continue his preaching," Hilary said, taking a deep breath.

"Who takes the services in the village when he is away."

"The vicar from the next parish comes once a month but" — again that little breathless pause before she rushed on — "I'm afraid not many people in our parish go to church. They say they can hear Father on the radio or what they call the 'telly'." She chuckled. "When Father is home, he visits every cottage, of course. They all respect him very much."

But do not like him, Philip thought instantly. "He preaches well?"

Again that small pause as if Hilary was thinking and not sure if she should say it. "His sermons frighten ME. He is an idealist and thinks there is only right and wrong. Mother thinks it is worse to be cruel to a child or a dog than to steal but Father expects so much of people and is always being disappointed. He is very hard to live up to — " He heard a soft little sigh. "That's why he was so upset when my sister eloped."

She told him about that. About her lovely gay sister who always wanted to be an actress but Father said NO. Who then worked for a lawyer in the nearby market town and who met a South African by chance. "They fell terribly in love. It was most awfully romantic. I was only fifteen and still at school. I never saw him. They had eloped by the time I came home. Father never forgave them."

"Yet he's letting you come out?"

"That's Mother."

The chatter round them was slowly dying down and Philip stifled a yawn. But he knew that this girl was very wide awake — that if she was to sleep, she must talk herself out. Why was he worrying about her? Just because she had a forlorn look as well as an elfin charm? Because she was so unaffected, so genuinely friendly, making no attempt to flirt with him? He had never met such a girl before. That was all it was. He was sorry for her.

She told him that her mother had inherited money — but that her husband,

19

the Reverend George Dale, handled it, for he did not think women capable of handling money wisely. He saw an inheritance as a sacred trust and believed the money should be used for the good of mankind and that they should live as cheaply as they could. "When my sister wrote that she was going to have a baby, Mother said we must help her. I had a lot of fun buying baby clothes and things and sending them out and Mother sent a cheque. My sister was very grateful. Mother wanted to send her more but Father said it was a man's duty to keep his wife." She went on as if quite unaware of the inconsistency of such a remark from her father. "Then recently my sister wrote that she was going to have an expensive operation and that another baby was on the way, that domestic help was terribly expensive and she did not know what to do. She might have to park Jackie — that's my nephew — and go to the nearby town. Mother hated the idea of her leaving her husband — she says that's how trouble starts — and she persuaded Father to let me come out." She gave a little jump of excitement in her seat. "That's why I'm here."

He tried to stifle a yawn but without much success.

"I'm boring you," Hilary said quickly. "Oh, I am sorry, I know I always talk too much."

In the darkness he found her hand and squeezed it gently. "Don't be an ass. If I'd been bored, I would soon have shut you up. But perhaps we should be quiet now — nearly everyone else seems to be asleep."

Hilary twisted in her seat. There were grunts and snores from the darkness. A baby whimpered a little.

She pulled the rug up to her chin and shivered. Odd that it was so cold now and yet it had been so hot. "Good night," she whispered.

"Good night."

She closed her eyes, never expecting to sleep. She awoke — battling with fear — the plane was falling, twisting and turning, the earth rushing up to meet them. . . .

Vaguely she was aware of someone soothing her — someone who put an arm round her shoulders, pressed her head down, put a warm hand on hers. Instantly her fear left her. She was safe. She relaxed and, in a moment, was sleeping dreamlessly.

★ ★ ★

They were rescued the following afternoon. It was a long hot day with the inside of the plane like a furnace and the shade of the trees unbearable because of the vicious ants and the thought of snakes falling from the branches. A long irksome day with throats getting drier, headaches worse, tempers rising, and a thousand small pinpricks becoming intolerable annoyances. The children were fretful, the babies echoed their mother's fears and cried incessantly, the blonde hostess looked harassed, for people kept asking when the rescuers would come, and how could she know?

Hilary kept away from Philip as unobtrusively as she could. She had been acutely embarrassed when she awoke that morning to find herself lying in his arms. She had looked up at his face, relaxed in

22

sleep, and felt a strange sensation. This was a good man, she had thought in that first moment of wakefulness. A man who can spare time to be kind to a lonely girl. A man who must surely be married and a father. How else would he have understood her need?

She moved out of his arms and went down the aisle of the plane to the cloakroom, before he awoke. The water was rationed so there was no hope of a wash and when she came back from combing her hair and doing her mouth, the mother of the twins was in despair with her two fractious boys, and only too glad of Hilary's assistance.

They heard sounds of the rescuers long before they saw them and the passengers were waiting, grouped round the end of the sandy strand before the first burly man came out of the trees, grinning at them. He had a gang of Africans who were chopping down branches, sawing trees. They chanted as they worked, shouting and laughing. Then they heard the bulldozer. Slowly, so very slowly, it seemed to the waiting, thirsty, hot travellers a way was cleared and several huge lorries came bouncing and jerking over the sand.

Then there was chaos! Everyone rushed to grab a place, remembered their luggage and rushed back to the plane, only to be told by the weary hostess that they need not worry about their luggage, they would be taken to an hotel for the night and their luggage sent direct to the airport to which they would travel tomorrow. They would just need things for the night. Hilary stood to one side and by the time she had got one of her suitcases, she found that she and Philip were the last to board the lorries. They had to sit on the floor in a very small space. He put his arm round her in the most natural way and they sat there, being jerked and jolted as the lorry went over the dry sand, bounced over tree branches, and came on to a bad earth road with deep sand at the corners, so that they skidded. Philip was tall and could catch glimpses of the scenery. He was glad Hilary seemed content to rest against his shoulder, her eyes half closed. It was steep — spectacularly dangerous — as they rocked their way down the twisting narrow road that led down the side of the mountain to the valley far below. He thought Hilary was sleeping but she was not. She was savouring the feel of his arm, the faint scent of his jacket, a mixture of tobacco and something else. Her mouth and eyes were full of dust and her hair felt clogged with it. Dimly she heard the other occupants of the lorry grumbling — the *camaraderie* of danger that they had shared when the plane force-landed, was now gone.

At last they reached a town. Not very big but the bright neon lights in the streets and the lighted shops were a welcome sight to most of the weary travellers. They were off-loaded — like cattle, as one of the passengers grumbled — at an hotel and Hilary's legs were so stiff that Philip had to lift her out of the lorry. She blinked stupidly as they stood in the brightly lighted foyer of the hotel and waited to sign the book. Philip walked with her to her room and smiled down at her as he opened her door.

"Look, Hilary — " How naturally he said the name and how lovely it sounded, she thought, blinking up at him. "Have a good hot bath and then put on a pretty frock. I see there's a dance on here tonight." He frowned, remembering her stern background. "HAVE you got a pretty frock?"

She felt herself colour under the thick dust. "Of course, Mother made me buy a cocktail frock, she said I was sure to need it in Africa."

He chuckled. "She's right — that's one thing you will need, anywhere in Africa. Well, be as quick as you can. I'm in the mood for dancing."

So was she, she found to her surprise, an hour later. She had soaked in a very hot bath, changed into clean undies and put on the coral pink nylon frock she had chosen out of the frocks her mother had sent for 'on approval'. It had a demure neck but was sleeveless and the waist nipped in, accentuating her slenderness. What luck she had short hair for she could wash it in the bath and rub it almost dry with the towel, only then pressing in its natural waves with her fingers. Luckily too, she had put her best nylon stockings and her high-heeled shoes in her night-case — her guardian angel must have prompted her, she thought with a breathless wave of excitement.

She felt a little nervous as she went down the stairs but Philip was waiting. He came to meet her, so tall, so impressive-looking, his voice significant as he looked at her and said: "Good girl — we've time for a drink before dinner. I hate rushing things, don't you?"

She did not like to tell him that this was the first time a man had taken her out to dinner or bought her a drink. She sipped it nervously but Philip had guessed it was her first and had merely bought her a sweet sherry. He watched her face as she sipped it as if it might be poison and he chuckled inwardly as he wondered what Fenella would say if she could see him.

Most of the passengers ate dinner hastily and retired to bed, but many local people had come in to the hotel for the monthly dance and the ballroom was gay with balloons and coloured streamers. As Philip put his arm round Hilary, she was afraid lest she prove unable to dance with him. Once again, she blessed her good fortune — being so short, she had taken the part of 'lady' even at school dances, and she found no difficulty in following his steps.

It was a magic evening, the kind that happens once in a lifetime, she reminded herself, a little afraid of the emotion she felt when she looked at Philip. Tomorrow they would fly on to Entebbe, where she would take another plane to Monsimbe and must say goodbye to him, never to see him again.

She was very conscious of her unaccustomed high heels as they went up the stairs together but it was worth having feet that ached! The lights in the corridor were dim, most of the doors had shoes, dusty with sand, outside them. At Hilary's door they paused. She looked up at him, unconsciously lifting her mouth invitingly as she said:

"I don't know how to thank you for a most wonderful evening. I'll never forget it."

He looked down into the young ardent eyes, saw the unconscious invitation of her lips. "Neither shall I," he said gently and bent and kissed her. His arms were warm round her and her whole body responded to the embrace. He felt the warmth of the young lips, the way she put her arms for a brief moment round his neck, the way she stepped back the instant he released her.

"I shouldn't have done that," he said with swift contrition as he saw the colour in her cheeks. Probably the first time she had ever been kissed. It should have been by someone of her own age, someone free to love and appreciate her.

"Don't be sorry," Hilary said, with that now familiar breathless rush of words. "Don't be sorry. I'm glad." She slipped into her room and he was gazing at the closed door. He went on staring at it for a moment and then walked down to his own room, yawning, thinking of bed and yet not regretting the evening. It had been strangely restful; no spoiled glamour-girl by his side gazing expectantly round the crowded room for admiring eyes, being petulant, demanding constant attention. Hilary had enjoyed herself and had let him see it. Which was something few women did.

2

THE next day, Hilary did not see Philip until the plane landed at Entebbe. In the morning, Hilary had breakfasted with the harassed mother of the twins and had begun to help her with them, so that it was natural for her to sit with them in the cream bus that drove furiously towards the nearest airport. In the plane, Hilary found herself sitting near one of the young mothers whose baby was fretful. At Entebbe, most of the passengers went through the Customs and vanished but Hilary had to wait for another plane to take her to Monsimbe. As she sat, rather forlornly alone, Philip Randel came up to her.

"This is where we part," he said and smiled down at her. "I hope you find your sister well. I suppose you are waiting to be met?"

She looked up at him. "I'm going on to Monsimbe," she said.

He looked startled. In the background, the metallic voices resounded from the tannoy, there was chatter, the reverberating noise of plane engines being revved up; but they were in a quiet corner alone.

"You're going to Monsimbe?" he said slowly. "But . . . what is your sister's name?"

"Fay Norton," Hilary said in that breathless eager little voice he now knew so well. "Do you know her?"

He looked down at the slight girl whose face was tilted up to his so excitedly, saw the huge dark eager eyes.

"Yes, I know Fenella Norton," he said very slowly, the words feeling as if they were being dragged from him.

Hilary's face crinkled into laughter. "That's Fay. She always hated the name of Fay and said if she ever went on the stage, she would be called Fenella. I wonder if that's what Dan calls her."

Philip stared down at Hilary, his eyes puzzled. She had struck him as such an honest, unaffected person and yet. . . .

Hilary sensed instantly the change on his face. She wondered if he and the

Nortons disliked one another. It was obvious that Philip Randel was none too pleased at the discovery that Hilary was going to his neighbourhood, to stay with people he knew.

A brassy voice blared over the tannoy. Philip turned his head and then said curtly: "That's our plane. Where's your luggage?"

They sat side by side in the smaller plane that was taking them the last part of their journey. They sat in an uncomfortable silence; uncomfortable for Hilary because she liked him and it seemed so out of character for him to suddenly freeze like this and look at her with hostile eyes. She could think of nothing she had said that might have annoyed him. Uncomfortable for Philip — for out of Hilary's own mouth, she had proved herself to be a liar. The last thing he would have expected of her. The silence became unbearable in its length. Hilary broke it with an effort.

"I sent my mother a cable. I thought she might have heard news of our forced landing."

"Good idea," he said curtly. Then he

turned to her, his eyes accusing. "If your mother is an invalid, who is looking after her now?"

"Oh, but she isn't an INVALID," Hilary said quickly. "Did I give you that impression? It's just that she suffers from anaemia and gets easily tired. We have a good maid — Mother has had her for twenty years — and she runs the house. Then we have two neighbours who pop in and out every day. All the villagers love Mother — though she is often very abrupt with them. She can't bear people who just moan and do nothing about improving their conditions."

"I see." He was looking down, now, at the sandy bush below, with the thousands of thorn trees dotted about. Soon be home, he thought, stretching his legs. "How long do you plan to stay out here?"

"I don't know." That was something her mother had refused to discuss. "Six months, I should think, or longer if Fay needs me. Tell me," Hilary overcame her sensitiveness and turned to him eagerly, "how is Fay? Is she as lovely and as gay as ever? I always thought there was no one like Fay. When she comes into a room, everyone looks at her. I think she's wonderful." Her breathless voice ceased abruptly as he turned to look at her with cold grey eyes.

"Yes," he said harshly, "she is just as lovely but I would not say as gay. She hasn't had an easy life out here and I don't think she is happy."

He regretted his words as he saw the way the happiness was wiped off the girl's face. "But," Hilary hesitated, "but I thought she loved Dan so much."

"It's a very different life out here," Philip said, his voice still harsh, "as you'll find. A lot of people can't stand up to it — they break under the strain."

"And Fay is one of those?" The blood had gone out of her face, her eyes seemed to be larger than ever.

Philip frowned. "I wouldn't say that. But I would say that life hasn't come up to all her youthful expectations," he said with deliberate sarcasm, watching the flame of colour rush over her pale face.

"Her letters — "

"It's easy enough to write letters — "

"But that's just it — it was the things

she didn't say in her letters that made Mother feel I should come out. It wasn't only the operation Fay has to have, or the lack of domestic help, or who would look after Jackie — Mother said she felt from Fay's letters that she needed one of her family with her. Do you think that Mother sensed that Fay was unhappy? She never says so in her letters but they're always very short and nothing ever seems to have happened. She always says, 'There is no news'."

It was time to fasten seat-belts as the plane had ceased to rocket and buck in the air pockets and was steadily losing height. Hilary looked out of the window eagerly but there wasn't much to see. Sandy brown ground with funny little trees and shrubs dotted all over it. They were circling round a few buildings now, dropping lower and lower and then, with a gentle bump, they touched ground and the plane ran slowly down the runway.

Hilary lost sight of Philip as they disembarked. She went into the rather bare hangar-like building that housed the airport's restaurant and offices and looked eagerly for Fay. Their mother would have cabled and Fay would have found out about the delayed arrival. Hilary and Philip were the only two passengers leaving the plane and she saw him talking to one of the officials. She deliberately turned her back and settled down, determined not to be impatient. There were a thousand reasons why Fay was not there — perhaps the chief one being that Fay had absolutely no idea of time.

She was aware of someone standing, looming over her, but it was an effort to turn her head. Her heart sank as she saw Philip Randel standing there, his face angry.

"There's no one to meet you," he said accusingly.

Quite suddenly she felt very tired and desperately homesick. The shock of the forced landing was just beginning to make itself felt; Philip's unexpected hostility, and now no welcome seemed the last straw. To her dismay, she felt the tears welling up into her eyes.

"Don't worry," she snapped, hoping he would not see her tears. "I'm not a child. I can look after myself. Mother was cabling Fay and she'll be here to meet me."

"Cables can get lost and," Philip's face softened for a moment, "I don't know if it is a new habit of Fenella's — I mean Fay's — but she has no idea of time."

Hilary managed an uneasy laugh. "She never had."

He picked up her suitcase. "No point," he said briskly, "in you sitting here and waiting indefinitely. I can run you out to their place. It's only about twenty miles from where I live. If we meet them on the way, I can hand you over."

"I hate to be a nuisance," Hilary said unhappily as she followed him out of the building.

"Not your fault," he said curtly. Which did not make it any easier to endure.

A tall African came running, in starched khaki shorts and shirt, with long bare legs, terminating in tiny nylon socks and highly polished brown brogues. His face was one huge smile and he greeted Philip excitedly.

The only word Hilary picked up was *Bwana* which apparently meant Sir. They wedged themselves into the front seat of a green Rover, with Hilary between the African driver and Philip.

She looked round eagerly as they moved fast over the flat road full of *dongas* and ruts, the Rover dipping and swaying alarmingly. There was nothing much to admire — just miles of sandy coloured soil with clumps of bushes and oddly-shaped trees whose branches spread out like the twisting spikes of umbrellas. The earth road eventually came to a straggling town of single-storeyed tin-roofed buildings, most of them looking as though a good coat of paint was needed, with small gardens full of tropical flowers. These interested Hilary most as she saw the luxuriant growth of purple bougainvillaea climbing over porches or the deep red of poinsettias with their pointed bare branches and huge bushes of scarlet hibiscus.

The houses became stores — one-storeyed buildings with huge windows packed with clothes and saucepans and shoes, all jumbled up together. It was very hot indeed and there seemed a shimmering haze over the road. There were a lot of Africans in the little town, sauntering along or forming small groups, from whom shouts of laughter drifted. A few rackety old cars were parked outside the stores.

"Monsimbe," Philip said briefly. "Our shopping centre."

"No — really?" Hilary began to laugh, saw the look on his face and stopped. "Is it far from Fay's?"

"About thirty miles," Philip said gruffly. He sat back, arms folded, his eyes fixed on the road ahead, his mouth stern.

Hilary sat very quietly, gazing ahead, trying not to wonder what it would feel like to live thirty miles from the village they had just passed. However did you housekeep? Would they have a refrigerator? How did you manage about milk?

A thousand questions bothered her for if Fay went into hospital the housekeeping would devolve on Hilary. She had often taken over the ordering and planning at home, for her mother believed a girl needed practical experience of that sort, but it would be very much harder here. At home, you could run down to the village store if you ran out of butter.

Here, it was quite, quite different.

The scenery changed a little. Perhaps the bushes grew closer, the trees looked more evil with their huge thorns sticking out. The road wound on and on but they could see little ahead, many of the corners being almost blind because the biggest trees seemed to choose the edge of the road, preferably on a turn. But they met no traffic at all. Twisting her head once, she saw the enormous cloud of dust being flung up behind them. She felt hot and dusty and rather miserable. She had felt in the short time she had known Philip Randel that they had become friends — now he was almost an enemy. Why? Was he afraid that she would make too much of that good-night kiss? Did he think that living so near him, she might cling, might try to make more of the little interlude than it deserved. She writhed inwardly, her pride hurt. Had he such a poor opinion of her? The journey seemed endless — she tried to reckon how long it would take to do thirty miles on such a bad road. Once she glanced at the speedometer and was shocked to see that they were doing a steady sixty. She glanced at the driver's face. He was grinning widely as he drove, looking very pleased with life. She glanced even more swiftly at Philip. He was leaning back, his eyes closed, two deep lines running down from his nose to his mouth. He looked tired and unhappy.

Imperceptibly, the scenery changed. The road wound upwards and then dipped — they went through a drift of water and scrambled up a steep bank opposite. Farther on, they drove over a concrete causeway that crossed a much wider, deeper river. There were bigger trees now, but still no houses.

"We're nearly there," Philip said abruptly. "Just up that hill."

She looked ahead and saw a slight rising, hardly large enough she would have thought to be called a hill. She was thankful the nightmare journey was nearly over. She felt caked with dust, her head throbbed from the heat in the Rover, her body was bruised by the jerking and shaking.

"The house is on the other side of this *koppie*," Philip told her.

The road twisted and turned, making a great deal of the shallow rise as it wound its way through an avenue of what seemed to be recklessly tossed boulders. These lay about higgledy-piggledy so that the track snaked between and around them. The heat reflected from the huge stones was terrific. The track was little more than two deep ruts in the red earth and then as they turned the corner, they climbed steeply for fifty yards and she saw that the *koppie*, as Philip called it, was higher than she first thought.

As if he could read her mind, he said curtly, "It's cooler up here and healthier. In the valley, there's malaria and other fevers."

They turned a corner and left the boulders behind. Now they were running along a road lined with small bushes.

Strong dark green bushes that pushed and jostled one another as if for pride of place, encroaching on the road so that they brushed the sides of the Rover. They turned another corner and she saw a building.

She thought at first it was a cow shed. It was just mud and wattle daub with a rusty red roof. And then she saw there were curtains at the windows and a thread of blue smoke rising from one chimney.

The Rover jerked to a standstill. Now she could see into the small porch that had obviously been added as an afterthought for it was the only part of the building that was thatched. There was a table with a chair on either side of it.

She jumped out of the Rover eagerly, not noticing Philip's offer of help, just as a huge black and white bull mastiff came lumbering round the building. His jowl swung as he walked, he had a ruff of black and white fur round his neck, his eyes blinked sleepily.

"That's Samson," Philip told her, just as an African came from behind the back of the building. A tall too-thin boy in grubby white shorts and shirt, he stared stupidly at Philip, who spoke to him sharply and told the driver to take out the suitcases from the back of the Rover.

Philip turned to Hilary. "Well, here you are." He spoke gruffly. "Your sister's resting but you'll soon wake her up. I'll say good-bye."

Hilary halted — she had been on her eager way into the house.

"Won't you come in?" she began and stopped as he stared down at her. "Thank you very much for bringing me," she went on, hesitantly, bewildered and hurt by the coldness in his eyes. "Fay couldn't have got the cable."

"I didn't think she would have got it, somehow," he said, "'bye." He snapped at the driver who swung into the driving seat, swung himself aboard and the Rover went swaying down the hill, leaving Hilary to stare after it, trying to read the meaning behind the significant way he had said: "I didn't think she would have got it."

At that moment, a clear voice said: "Philip — don't go . . . "

Hilary turned and saw her sister come running out. Hilary caught her breath. Fay was just as lovely as ever — with that heart-shaped face, the naturally golden hair, the deep blue eyes, the tall slim body, the long slender legs. Now she was wearing white shorts and a shirt hanging outside them, her hair was ruffled, her cheeks flushed as if she had been asleep.

And then she saw Hilary. Across her face ran a conflicting series of expressions but Hilary had no time to sort them out.

"Fay — Fay darling," she cried and ran forward eagerly. "It's heavenly to see you."

Fay's arms were warm and welcoming as the two sisters kissed. Then Fay held her sister away and gazed down at her. "But darling — "she hesitated. "Is Mother all right?" she asked sharply.

"Didn't you have her cable? She said she was sending you one . . . "

"Yes — " Fay said slowly. "She did, but she said nothing about you in it."

"What did she say?"

Fay smiled. The same old smile Hilary remembered so well and yet different. It was a smile of the mouth only, it did not seem to reach any other part of her face.

"She said: 'Am sending help immediately. Writing.' I thought she meant a cheque."

Hilary laughed. She was so glad to have reached her destination, she felt as if a weight, almost unbearable to carry, had been lifted.

"I'm the help while you have your op. and the baby — "The words suddenly died away as she stared at Fay. Fay, quite definitely, was not going to have a baby. Or if she was, not for months and months. She was as thin as a rake.

"Have you seen our fabulous view?" Fay was saying, ignoring the last remark, as she turned Hilary and pointed to the horizon. From where they stood, close to the *stoep*, they could see over the valley which stretched away, mile after mile of sandy soil, dotted with thorn trees. There was a shimmering haze of heat over it and Hilary was suddenly aware that she was dying for a cup of tea.

"It's beautiful," she said but there was no enthusiasm in her voice. Once more, she felt unbearably tired and homesick.

"Come inside and Petrus will fix us a cold drink," Fay said, leading the way through the porch and into a cool dark room.

Coming directly from the blinding, searing sunshine, Hilary blinked for a while before she could see properly. It was a small square room with three rather dilapidated armchairs grouped round a low table, with a radio on a shelf and an open cupboard showing glasses and a row of bottles.

"You look tired out — why didn't Philip stay? He is odd . . . " Fay was saying as she turned to the cupboard. She went to the doorway and shouted and a tall African with grizzled grey hair and a look that reminded Hilary absurdly of the *Uncle Tom* of her childhood books, came in, bearing a large frosted jug of water. He looked curiously at Hilary and Fay spoke to him easily in his own language. He smiled at Hilary and gave a little bow and said something.

"He says welcome — "Fay told her as she carefully poured out a drink. "I suppose you'd like iced passion fruit. Too early for you to want gin. Too early in the day, I mean. Dan says I should wait for the sun to go down but it takes such a hell of a time that I get fed up waiting," Fay went on.

Hilary was suddenly aware that her sister was nervous, that she was chattering away shrilly because she was trying to postpone an inevitable moment. Instantly Hilary felt better.

Fay brought the ice-cold golden drink and gave it to Hilary, looked down at her sister's affectionate eyes and ceased talking. She curled up in a chair, tucking her lovely slim legs under her and smiling.

"I can see you're puzzled."

"You're not going to have a baby?" Hilary asked bluntly.

Fay shook her head. She took a long draught of the drink in her hand. "Nor an operation," she said curtly.

Hilary sipped at her drink and the ice-cold liquid soothed her dry throat.

"Is Jackie all right?"

"There is no Jackie," Fay said. "There never was," she ended, her voice defiant. She gazed at Hilary. "I suppose you're shocked," she said scornfully.

Hilary's eyes roved round the shabby room and came back to Fay. "Should I be shocked?" she said mildly. "I'm just surprised."

Fay got up and began to prowl round the room, her face spoiled by a scowl. "I had to do something. There was no other way . . . ."

"No other way?"

"Look — "Fay came to stand in front of her, her hands on her hips, her face angry. "You always were so righteous. I know you despise me for telling lies, for deceiving Mother. I don't give a damn about Father — " her voice was hard. "I had no choice, Hilary. We were desperately poor — Dan had been ill — I didn't know which way to turn. He was mauled by a leopard and couldn't work for months. I had to have money. I knew Father would never send out money for Dan so — so I invented the baby."

Hilary took a long drink this time, remembering the hours she had spent choosing baby clothes for her little nephew, knitting, buying toys.

"What did you do with the things we sent out?" she asked dully.

"Sold 'em, of course," Fay said. She sat down opposite Hilary. "Look . . . " her voice became pleading for a moment. "After all it is OUR money, Hilary. Grandfather left the money to Mother but he always let us think that we — that you and I would benefit. It's Father . . . " her voice hardened again, "Father, with his craze for helping mankind — so that he will become famous for his charity. His charity," she said scornfully, "when the money is Mother's and ours. It wasn't stealing . . . " she went on, "it is ours by right and if I had to cheat Father, well, I'm not sorry . . . " she stopped abruptly.

Hilary stared at her, at the face now contorted by tears and anger, and she knew that Fay was sorry. Very sorry, indeed.

"Oh, darling," she said, "I do understand. It's just that . . . "

" . . . That you can't bear to deceive Mother. I know."

There was a miserable silence. Fay went on. "I thought I was being so clever. I thought having succeeded once, I could do it again. And instead of sending me money, Mother has sent YOU . . . " her voice broke and she began to laugh. "Isn't it funny? I wanted money to buy us food and all she sent is an extra mouth to feed."

Hilary moved quickly, kneeling by her sister, her arm round her. "But she is sending you money," she said. "I know she is. I probably came faster than the mail."

Fay turned to her. "Are you very shocked, Hilary? Can you really understand?" Her voice was low. "You've led such a sheltered life. How can you know what it is to have a husband like Dan . . . " She stopped. "I mustn't say things like that — " she dabbed at her eyes. "Dan can't help it. I ought to have seen what he was like but I was so young . . . " She saw Hilary's face and hugged her suddenly. "Forget it, Hilary. Dan is a darling, and I am very happy, so do stop worrying about it. It shows on that funny little face of yours so plainly."

She jumped to her feet. "I'll soon rig up a bed for you but it's only a small room. Like a wash?" She shouted to the kitchen and Petrus came running with a jug of hot water.

Fay led the way through the door and into a bedroom — it had a low double bed covered by a patchwork quilt — through that room, into a narrow cell of a room with a barred open window high in the wall and a small rug.

"We've a camp bed packed away you can have. The bathroom is outside." Out through a narrow door and into what was obviously a pantry. Cool, gloomy, with stone floor and shelves packed with tins of food, a small paraffin refrigerator and a locked cupboard. Out again — all the rooms leading in and out of one another, to an earth yard and a crazy-looking hut with a tilted tin roof and the smell of frying onions drifting from it.

"That's the kitchen," Fay pointed. "Petrus is our cookboy — Dan picked him years ago down in Swaziland so he speaks a different lingo. Then there is Carl, he brought in your cases, and I have a garden boy, Simon." She led the way to a small rondavel and flung open the door. There was a tin hip bath there with a rather Heath-Robinson sort of contraption above which was a shower. "Cold water, only — " Fay laughed, "but out here that is welcome!" There was an enamel bowl on a wooden table and a very primitive lavatory. "None of the amenities of civilization," Fay mocked. "Don't know how you'll like it."

Hilary drew a deep breath. "I'm longing for a wash," she said in a matter-of-fact voice, not trusting herself to say any more.

After she was alone, she washed quickly, plunging her face again and again into the cold water she got from the shower. As she dried herself, she looked round wonderingly. Fay, who had loved luxury and had grumbled about the rectory's primitive sanitary arrangements, seemed quite satisfied with this. How had Fay changed? And why?

As she was drying, she remembered something; it was as if her heart stood still. Now she knew why Philip Randel had changed when he discovered that he knew her sister. He would know that Fay had no child, was expecting no baby.

3

WHEN Hilary returned to the house, she saw that already the bed was in her bedroom, made up and with a pink cover on it. Fay was in the sitting-room, pouring out tea, welcoming her with a smile.

"I hadn't realised how much I missed you all until now," she said. "It's lovely to see you. I'm sure you're dying for a cup of tea. If I'd known you were coming . . . " She laughed excitedly and rubbed her nose. The little familiar gesture warmed Hilary's heart. This was the Fay she remembered.

Over tea, Fay wanted to know all about the journey. "I wish Philip had come in," she said a little wistfully, "we see so few people here that any face is better than no face. Did you meet him in England?"

"Oh no, only on the plane. We had to make a forced landing." Hilary told her sister the whole story. "I doubt if I would have met Philip but for the fact that he was sitting next to me and saw I was scared stiff — ”

“Poor you. I know how scared you’ve always been of everything. Haven’t you grown out of it?” Fay asked sympathetically. “It must have been very frightening. Was he nice to you?”

“Kind. And reassuring. He made me talk — ” Hilary’s hand flew to her mouth. “That reminds me, Fay. It’s just too terrible. I told him I was coming out to help you with Jackie and the baby — he must know that’s not true. How can I ever face him again?”

Fay looked concerned. She curled up in the chair, clasping her knees.

“We’ll have to think of something. I’d hate him to know I’d made it up to get money out of father. You see, Philip is important to us. He could sack Dan.”

“But he wouldn’t — ” Hilary was shocked.

Fay shrugged. “He’s a queer cuss. Haven’t you noticed that? Moody . . . Changeable. He’s got a strict code — he thinks lying is despicable. I’d hate him to look at me with those queer cold eyes of his . . . ”

Hilary shuddered. She knew just what Fay meant, for that was exactly how Philip had looked at her.

"What can we say?" she asked despairingly.

Fay jumped up. "Don't let's fret now — we'll cross that bridge when it comes. Some more tea? I'll think of something." She poured another cup. "I suppose he was sorry for you. He always is protective to young things. I sometimes wish I was a young thing," she laughed, but Hilary, looking sharply at her, detected a serious note behind it.

"Where's Dan," she asked, to change the subject.

Fay was roaming round the room, now, plumping up a cushion, straightening one of the silver cups that marched along the mantelpiece.

"Out hunting a lion. A man-killer."

She said it so casually that Hilary looked at her, expecting to see that Fay was teasing her. But Fay was serious.

"Isn't that very dangerous?" Hilary asked, not sure whether to believe Fay or not.

Fay looked at her. "Of course it is.

This is a wounded lion so he has to be killed. The news came through and Dan had to go. As a rule Philip gets the news first and decides which of his men must go after the lion. Dan felt it was his responsibility. But don't get het up, darling, it's all in a day's work to Dan. The great white hunter . . . " she said, with a sneer in her voice.

Petrus, the houseboy, came padding in on his bare, pink-soled feet, and said something to Fay who answered him in his own language. Then she looked at Hilary.

"Stop looking so anxious — Petrus tells me Dan has got his lion and is bringing it home."

"But . . . but how does he know?"

Fay laughed. "Bush telegraph. They know things hours before we do despite the telephone."

"Have you got a phone? Could I send a cable to Mother . . . " Hilary said eagerly.

"Of course . . . " Fay stood still in the middle of the room and looked down at her sister. "What are you going to tell her, Hilary, or haven't you thought?"

Hilary looked up at her sister's lovely face and saw the anxiety there. "Oh, Fay, what must I do?"

Fay came to sit on the arm of her chair. "I know how you feel, Hilary," she said affectionately. "You always were such a truthful little prig, bless you. But what good will it do to tell Mother the truth? She'll be bitterly hurt to think that I could lie to her and as for Father — " her voice hardened, "we'd never see a penny of that money that's rightfully ours." She jumped up, began to pace about like a caged lioness. "That's what makes me so mad, Hilary. Grandfather meant us to enjoy the money. He earned every penny of it himself. He built up that business from rock bottom, it was his whole life. He never meant that money to lie in a bank, to be spent on weaklings who haven't the guts to make a living for themselves. He never meant it to be handled by a Bible-thumping . . . "

"Fay," Hilary cried out, shocked at the violence in Fay's voice.

Fay looked a little ashamed. "Sorry, darling, I forgot you still see Father through the eyes of a child. I dare say

58

he does preach well and I am sure he is a good man by his standards but they are not mine. He hasn't an ounce of human kindness in his body. If he had, would he have cast me off like that? Wouldn't he have accepted the fact that I was old enough to know my own mind — I was twenty-one and no fool — wouldn't he have helped us to make a success of our marriage, not done his best to wreck it? You don't know — but I wrote to him, asking him to forgive my elopement and suggesting that Dan and I came home before we left England. He wrote back an icy letter saying that I had chosen my path and must abide by my own choice, that he had no desire to see me again." She stopped as Hilary gave a little cry. "Do you wonder that I resent him — that I feel we have a right to the money?"

She paced round the room, her long graceful strides making it seem smaller than it was.

"Look — if Father had any human love in him, would he dump Mother in that desolate huge freezing rectory while he goes off all round the country, being treated like a V.I.P.? He knows she needs proper treatment, that she should have good food, a warm home, comfort, someone to nurse her but no, he prefers to let her grow weaker and weaker . . . ”

"Oh no, Fay," Hilary burst out, unable to bear it any longer. "I'm sure you are wrong. He does love Mother — ”

"In his own way." Fay stopped walking and stared down at her sister. "Well, what are you going to do? Back me up in my harmless deception or play the game Father's way . . . ”

Before Hilary could answer, they heard shouting and the sound of a car. Fay turned to the front door, Hilary close behind her. Up the steep ascent to the house, came a Land Rover, it seemed packed with *boys*. Africans of every size and shape, some in ragged khaki shorts and shirts, others with a strip of cloth tucked across their bodies, over and under one arm, with an animal skin hanging down from their waists.

The Rover jerked to a stop and a short, broad-shouldered man clambered out. He wore a very sweat-stained battered sun-hat, khaki shorts and shirt and he shouted at the Africans, who immediately jumped out, still shouting excitedly and began to drag something out of the back of the Rover.

Then Dan turned to his wife — and saw Hilary. He looked startled.

"Come and meet your sister-in-law," Fay said.

Dan walked towards them. He walked with a sort of roll, his shoulders well back, his square chin jutting out pugnaciously. His eyes were cold though he smiled.

"No kidding? How did you get here?" He looked at Hilary.

"I flew out," she said and held out her hand. "It's nice to meet you, Dan," she said simply, meaning it.

He looked at his hand, wiped it on his shorts, and shook her hand solemnly. "Just lion blood," he said casually. "Quite a beast. Want a look?"

The lion lay sprawled on the ground; its dignity vanished. It was a huge monster, Hilary thought, as she gazed down at it, with a great ruff round its neck. Its eyes were closed — there was a small hole drilled between them. Dan stooped and lifted a paw that fell heavily to the ground as he let it go.

"See — the leg was broken. The poor devil must have suffered a hell of a lot of pain. No wonder he had to kill whatever he could get." His voice was so compassionate that Hilary glanced at him curiously.

He looked up, caught her gaze and slowly coloured. "Just because I shoot animals, doesn't mean I'm a killer," he said truculently. "I know it's my living but I assure you I get no kick out of it. Out of the hunting, yes — but not the killing. This was different — he was a menace and had to be killed." He straightened. "Well, what about a drink?" He shouted some orders and the *boys* seized the lion and carried it round the house. Now Dan looked at Hilary more closely.

"You're not a bit alike."

She met his gaze steadily. "Everyone says that."

"Well," he asked. "What do you think of me — now you've met me?" he spoke defiantly.

Hilary found herself beginning to

laugh. "Why, Dan, what a silly question." Without thinking, she took his arm. "I'm sure you're dying for a drink. How can I know what I think of you when we've only just met. Ask me in ten days time . . ."

His stiff face began to relax. "Will you tell me the truth if I do that?"

She laughed up at him, her eyes large in her small pointed face.

"Yes, Dan, I promise to tell you. I'm a very truthful person, you know."

"Good." He led the way into the house. Fay was pouring drinks. "How come your sister is honouring us with a visit?" he asked, as he took the long glass she handed him.

Fay glanced at him without a smile. "Mother thought she needed to see something of the world and this is as good a place to start as any."

Dan sank into a chair and tilted his glass. He gave a sigh after he had drained it, wiped his mouth with the back of his hand, and handed the glass back to Fay, who stood by his chair waiting. "That certainly was good," he said slowly. "It must have been a bit of a shock to have your sister walk in like that, Effie." He spoke casually but Hilary sensed that it was a deliberate casualness. And noticed that Dan called her 'Effie'. So Fay had three names. Fay. Fenella and Effie.

"Mother said she was sending a cable — " Hilary said quickly.

Fay's back was turned as she was filling Dan's glass. "Probably arrive three months from now. You know what our mail is . . ."

Dan turned to look at Hilary. At the same moment Petrus and Carl came into the room, carrying lamps with rounded globes. They placed one on the table — one on a shelf, and pumped carefully, the lamps sizzling and then gradually flaring up into a harsh white light. The room looked immediately different, not quite so shabby, nor so small, for the corners were in deep shadow.

"Couldn't have been much of a welcome for you," Dan said slowly, "landing at the airport and with no one to meet you. Howd'ya find your way here?"

Again she had the sense that Dan wanted to ask more direct questions and was deliberately keeping a curb on his tongue.

"Philip brought her," Fay said.

The hand that held his glass tightened. Hilary chanced to be looking at it and she saw the muscles tighten, the skin turn white.

"That was nice for her." Now there really was a significant note in Dan's voice. Hilary plunged into the conversation — afraid of something, yet not sure of what.

"I met him on the plane. I didn't know he knew you until he said good-bye to me at Entebbe and . . . "

"Their plane made a forced landing," Fay put in, "and apparently Philip took compassion on her. He saw she was scared."

Dan looked at Hilary quickly. "Don't blame you," he said gruffly. "I loathe the things myself. Anyone hurt?"

"Oh no. Just that we were there a day and a half — there wasn't much food and less water and it was frightfully hot."

"I bet it was . . . " Dan paused and she sensed the question in the air.

"Mr. Randel was sitting next to me in the plane and he saw I was frightened," Hilary struggled on, wondering why a simple little account should be so difficult to give. "They warned us we would make a forced landing and . . . and . . . "

"Philip took pity on you," Fay supplied.

"He talked to me — made me think of other things. Then — then when we had landed, we walked a bit with the others. There was the most incredibly lovely view and then . . . "

"Then?" Dan held out his empty glass towards Fay with a peremptory movement. To Hilary, it was a surprise to see how meekly Fay accepted and refilled it.

"Well, then — then I helped someone who had small twin boys and — and we waited and waited and next day, we were rescued. We went by lorry to a town where we spent the night and the next day, were taken to an airport and flown to Entebbe. There Mr. Randel said good-bye to me and then we discovered we were both going to Monsimbe and — and at Monsimbe, he found there was no one to meet me so he said he would drop me off as it wasn't far out of his way."

"He sounds pretty ungracious about

it," Dan commented. "Not like our gallant Philip . . ."

Fay put her glass down with a little clatter on the table. "He was in one of his moods, apparently. He just dumped Hilary at the door and went off. I didn't see him."

"Pity," Dan said sarcastically. There was a silence. Slowly he stretched his legs and yawned. "It's good to be home," he said unexpectedly.

Samson came lumbering in from the kitchen and went to lean against Hilary. He looked up at her, his eyes winking as she stroked him.

"Samson accepted you?" Dan asked. "That's a compliment."

There was a tight lump in Hilary's throat. She could sense the atmosphere in the room and it made her feel horribly embarrassed. She was almost afraid to speak in case she said the wrong thing.

Sitting there quietly, she thought of Dan calling Fay 'Effie' — and Philip Randel calling her 'Fenella'. Dan acted as if he was jealous of Philip. What did it all add up to, she wondered unhappily, remembering Philip's defence of Fay, his

67

remark that she had a hard life.

Dan stood up and took a pipe off the mantelpiece and began to fill it. Fay cried out. "Your leg — Dan. Didn't you know . . . "

Dan bent and Hilary could see a small wound with a mass of dried blood over it. "I'd forgotten," he said casually.

Fay was instantly on her feet. "It's too bad of you, Dan," she said angrily. "You should have told me at once and . . . "

He grinned at her. "Too many distractions, isn't every day we're honoured by a visit from one of your family." This time he was not being sarcastic for he looked over at Hilary with a friendly smile. "My wife does flap so," he said and sounded absurdly pleased about it.

Fay had rushed out of the room; in a moment she returned with bandages and bottles; Petrus came hurrying with a bowl of boiling water, and Fay was on her knees by her husband, looking angrily at him. "You make me mad, I could honestly slap you, Dan," she scolded. She looked over at Hilary. "I'm not flapping but every little wound on Dan turns septic and he just won't do anything about them. How'd you like to lose your leg?" she asked him furiously.

He chuckled. "I'd get a wooden one and next time a croc took a bite at me, I'd give him the leg to chew on."

"You're such a clot, you'd probably give him the wrong leg," Fay grumbled as she bathed the small wound.

They went on bickering and Hilary, clutching her nearly full glass, sat back in the shadows, content to be ignored. This sort of atmosphere was quite different and much more bearable. Dan was obviously lapping up the attention he was getting and Fay must be very much in love with him, or else she would not worry.

"If you didn't drink so much . . . " she was scolding now as she refilled his glass.

"Hark at who's talking. You can drink me under the table any time, my girl."

"You stink," she said abruptly. "It's time for you to shower or the dinner will be a cinder."

He drained his glass and obediently stood up, walking with his odd roll to the door of the bedroom.

"Incidentally," Fay called out, "you'd

better get used to going to the bathroom through the front door, else you'll be disturbing Hilary."

He stood in the doorway and grinned. "Hey, hope I remember. Look, Hilary, if you wake at the crack of dawn and see a huge figure lumbering through your room, don't think I plan to murder you. It'll just be that I've forgotten."

"Okay," she laughed.

There was a silence as he left them. "Well?" Fay said defiantly.

Hilary put down her glass carefully. "I like him," she said. "What had Father against him, Fay?"

"Nothing at all — except everything. Father was quite right but, all the same . . . " Fay stabbed out her cigarette viciously . . . "Dan had no background — his parents are divorced, he was brought up by his grandmother. He had no future. He's employed as a white hunter; that means to escort wealthy Americans and such like when they want to kill wild animals with a maximum of excitement and the minimum amount of danger. Sometimes he does quite well but we blue the whole lot on a trip to

Zanzibar or even Johannesburg. We've not a penny saved and if Dan were injured tomorrow, I'd have to find a job to support us," she finished bitterly.

"Did you know this when you met him?"

Fay looked at her. "Of course. Dan is no liar." There was a tiny pause. "I thought he was just the cautious type, not wanting me to expect too much but I saw Africa as a romantic place where the sun always shone and one picked gold up off the ground. I didn't realize there were months of rain and mist, tropical fevers, poisonous spiders, snakes . . . "

Dan stood in the doorway, washed, shaved, clad in immaculate grey trousers and a white shirt. "Please note, Hilary," he said, standing in front of her and bowing, "that I have put on a tie."

"I am honoured," she said.

"You should be," Fay said grimly and went out of the room. They heard her shouting for Petrus.

Dan sat down, kicked out his legs and smiled at her. "I bet you're dead tired," he said surprisingly.

It had an unfortunate effect. Hilary felt her eyes welling up with tears. She nodded, for she dared not trust her voice.

"Has it shocked you very much?" he went on. He waved his hand about vaguely. "This — this primitiveness, I mean. We're used to it but I guess that to anyone like you . . . "

She hated his having to feel apologetic. "Dan — of course it's different but . . . " If only she could think of the right words to say. "I don't think it matters if you're happy. I mean, at home, we are frightfully primitive. We have an enormous Rectory and all but a few rooms have to be shut up. We just haven't the furniture for them and it is so frightfully cold there."

"One thing, you won't be cold here. I'm glad," he went on, "glad you've come out. I hated like hell feeling I'd broken up Effie's home life. She's the kind that needs someone of her own around. I hope you stay a long time."

"Thanks," she began, gratified, as well as surprised.

Fay came in, catching the last words.

"She'll be bored stiff after three months. What is there for anyone young here?" she said bitterly.

Carl was clearing the table now, laying it, banging down the plates, making a great clutter.

"I thought you liked the life here," Dan said.

"Life!" Fay said sneeringly. "Existence you mean. It's all right for you, out in your beloved bush all day, hunting, tracking, shooting. You're free as air. You never think of me, cooped up in this miserable hovel and . . . "

He sat up. "Look, Effie, we've been through this before. Where the devil could I get a job that would pay as well as this? . . . "

"Where, indeed," she said bitterly. "Wherever you were you'd be a misfit, Dan, and you know it."

"That's a lie and . . . " Their voices were raised now. As if accustomed to such a scene, Carl went on laying the table calmly, clumping back in toeless tackies across the polished floor, bumping into a chair as he went, his face intent on the job.

73

Then Petrus stood in the doorway, a small gong in his hand. He hit it hard three times and said in a bland voice: "Deen-aire is sairved."

Dan and Fay stopped squabbling, remembered Hilary and showed by their faces that they had forgotten her. "Don't you admire our butler?" Fay said quickly.

Dan was arranging chairs round the table. "Come and get it, folks," he said. He grinned at Hilary and placed one of the lamps on the table. "I had a Frenchman stay with me once, we did a spot of film-making. He taught Petrus to announce dinner with a French accent and the boy has never forgotten it."

The awkward moment had gone. Now Dan dished up, handing Hilary a plate of meat, a heap of beautifully cooked rice, tinned peas, baked potatoes.

"Hope you like it. You'd call it venison — we call it Tommy-meat. I shot it a couple of days ago but don't worry, we've a very adequate fridge."

The bright light on the table showed all their faces in a strange way — accentuating shadows, making Fay look thin and haggard, Dan tired and unhappy. Hilary wondered how she looked. If she looked one third of how tired she felt, she must look an awful hag.

4

HILARY sat on the *stoep*, a long cool drink at her elbow, as she lifted the heavy binoculars to her eyes and searched the distant plain. Dan had lent them to her, saying there would be plenty of game but it might take her a while to learn to *see* it. They had such extraordinary powers of fading into the background, he said, you have to learn to look for the right thing, the slight movement, the way the light fell. Well, so far, she had seen nothing at all.

She lowered the binoculars and sipped her drink. She could hear Carl inside the room, on his knees, polishing the floor, giving that funny little off-key chant of his. Fay had gone to Monsimbe for the day. She had asked Hilary if she would care to go, and had spoiled the invitation immediately by adding that there was nothing to see there, anyhow, and she thought Hilary should rest.

Had she really been with them three

whole weeks? Hilary wondered, half-closing her eyes. The sun-glare on the distant plain made her feel quite dizzy — with the waves of heat vibrating across the sandy ground. The day after her arrival she had felt sick and had been plunged into a violent attack of what Fay called 'funny-tummy.' Fay had taken it calmly. Everyone new to the country had it, she said, and a lot of residents as well. She had a medicine that acted swiftly and had nursed Hilary with an extraordinary patience and to Hilary, a warming affection.

Hilary had felt very ill, feverish, thoroughly exhausted, and had been content to lie in bed, tossing, turning, being bathed with luke-warm water, her nightie and sheets being constantly changed, sleeping fitfully. The only thing that worried her was the incessant quarrelling that went on in the evenings and which the thin partition walls did nothing to hide. She told herself that it was just 'their way'; that probably all married couples went on like this, that behind it, they really loved one another. But it still worried her.

In a lucid moment, she had written a brief letter to her mother, saying she had arrived safely and that everyone was very well and she would write more later, but she was grateful to the illness for postponing her decision on what she must finally tell her mother. It troubled her terribly as she lay, hot and sweating under the thin sheet, the pains in her stomach making her double up, the sweat stand out on her head.

Her mother had never been a demonstrative woman, believing that emotion was a weakening thing, that you became too vulnerable and made others equally so if you allowed your affection to spill over. So Hilary and Fay had grown up with few caresses and little praise but all the time Hilary had known that their mother loved them with a fierce unselfish love that only wanted their future happiness. Hilary knew that her mother had grieved terribly about Fay — that she felt their father was wrong in his handling of the situation, hence her regular letters to Fay, her eagerness to send money and clothes when Fay asked for them, her decision to send

Hilary out to help Fay when she felt Fay needed someone by her. That love meant that it was almost impossible to lie to her.

Hilary knew that her mother would understand the situation and, while she might not approve of Fay's way of wording it, that she felt the money left by their grandfather should also be available for them. So why lie to her at all?

On the other hand, their mother loved their father deeply. Hilary knew that very well. They might see little of him, he might show little interest in them, but when he came home, it was as if a light was switched on inside her mother's face and she glowed, her eyes sparkling, her whole being charged with excitement because HE was there. This love was coupled with a deep loyalty which would not allow her mother to admit their father could be wrong. So she might, conceivably, feel she had to tell him that Fay had lied to them. That would, of course, be the end, Hilary thought worriedly. So she had just drifted, but now she was feeling better and stronger every day, and not much longer could the decision be postponed. What should she tell her mother? The truth — and Fay's reasons for her lies? Or lie like Fay and keep their mother in blissful ignorance?

Another thing that worried her was that Dan obviously knew nothing of Fay's fabrications. Perhaps, then, he did not know that their mother had sent out money. How would he react if he found out? It seemed to Hilary that he had a fierce pride; when he talked of money, it was different from the way Fay talked of it. Quite obviously Dan was content with his job and salary; and that he felt it was sufficient for their needs. Equally obvious was the fact that Fay saw him as a 'failure', that she had expected far more from him when she married him. Who was to say which was the wrong attitude? Hilary felt too weak and bewildered to attempt to solve the problem but there was no doubt that their constant bickerings made her life there uncomfortable. Added to this, too, was the feeling that although Fay was so affectionate, yet she resented Hilary's unannounced arrival and saw her as merely another mouth to feed. If only there had been something Hilary could do to earn her keep; if there had been a small Jackie to care for, or a future baby for whom to make clothes, it would have helped.

Sitting on the *stoep*, Hilary watched the Africans as they drifted by. There was an almost constant stream and she never tired of watching them. Some of the girls were very primitive with their hair piled high with mud on a support, others had heads of tiny tight little curls; others again, wore gay head squares in vivid crimsons or bright blues and lemon yellows. Some were dressed in European clothes, bright pink satin frocks or flowered cretonne; others in animal skins with the upper halves of their bodies bare. Some carried crimson umbrellas as sunshades, others seemed not to notice the merciless rays of the sun. The older women nearly all had babies strapped to their backs by thick blankets. Hilary pitied the small babies sweltering in the heat, the tiny legs stretched wide apart over the mother's back, but when she looked into their faces, none of them seemed distressed at all. Often she wondered at the laziness of the male Africans who strolled down the cart track with empty hands, followed by their wives, staggering under the huge loads on their heads, often having a baby strapped to the back, and a couple of small children tagging along behind. Dan's theory of the male African's laziness was that originally when danger stalked everyone's footsteps, it behoved the male to walk unhampered by loads so that he could defend his family. Hilary wondered if this was the true origin or if the male African was just a lazy creature. Fay thought the latter.

There were always Africans coming with things to sell. Naartjies, bananas, bead necklaces, even intricate crochet mats. Many of them attended Mission schools, Dan said, and there was no doubt that the standard of crochet and embroidery — for there were embroidered tea cloths for sale, as well — was very high. You could always tell a Mission-trained African, Dan also said, for both male and female gave a little bob when they handed you anything.

The sun blazed down and Hilary was grateful for the shade of the thatched porch. The days had drifted by, merging so imperceptibly that the three weeks had flown past, and as most of them had been spent on her bed, Hilary still felt she had only just arrived.

She felt restless sitting there, and wishing she had gone into Monsimbe with Fay. Even if there had been nothing to see, the effort might have done her good.

It was with relief she saw Dan's Rover come racing up the hill, sending up the usual cloud of dust. He came towards her, that same friendly grin on his face that he seemed to reserve for her. Even as she watched him, she found herself planning what she must write to her mother.

"I like Dan," she would write, and it was true. There were times when his bluntness shocked her; when his swearing amazed her, for never had she heard such language but she saw that he swore without real meaning behind the words, and there was no real anger behind his bickering with Fay.

"Hey." Dan greeted her now as he sat down by her side. Carl came running with an ice-cold drink. Dan's face was not good-looking but Hilary had long ago ceased to wonder what Fay, the difficult, hard-to-please Fay, had seen in him, for now she could see Dan's charm for herself. It lay in those odd features that seemed to have been thrown together — a big nose, rather full mouth, square chin with an unexpected dimple in it, the fair crew-cut hair and the very clear brown eyes that stared at you thoughtfully. It was his smile, Hilary had decided, that twisted the heart of you. It was an odd smile, starting up rather shyly as if he expected a rebuff, and then blossoming out into a huge grin. Now he gave her that grin and she added a little more mentally to her letter to her mother.

"He is a very nice person, kind, unexpected, quick to anger but soon over it. I like him very much," she would say.

"Where's your sister?" he asked now.

"Gone to Monsimbe."

He lifted those thick brows. "Why

84

didn't you go?" He gave her that clear thoughtful look that could be so disconcerting.

"I . . . " She was confused. She did not like to say that obviously Fay had not wanted her to go, yet that was the truth. "We felt that it was a bit too soon after my — my illness."

Still that clear thoughtful look. "The change would have done you good. We'll have to organize a few outings for you. We've some pretty decent neighbours — " he grinned again, "or perhaps not exactly neighbours, but all within a radius of thirty miles, and we must take you to see them. I'd like you to see something of the countryside while you're with us. Unfortunately you've come at a bad time. I may have to go off on safari any moment now."

Fay was late. Dan said he was hungry, so he and Hilary lunched alone on iced soup, fried venison and water melon. Fay came in just as they were having coffee.

She had gone into Monsimbe in their old car and had had engine trouble, hence her late return, she told them gaily as she played with her lunch. No, she wasn't hungry, she said rather irritably when Hilary commented on her lack of appetite. Monsimbe had been so hot — it always tired her out. As she sipped the hot black coffee, she looked at Dan, her eyes very bright.

"I hear it's settled about those Americans. They'll be here within a week."

Dan was frowning. "Who told you? I've only just had the news myself. Philip — I suppose . . . "

"Philip wasn't at the office. I called in for mail and Miss Phipps told me. She was very excited about it, said they were very nice people and that we would have fun."

Dan went on frowning. "We? You can't come, now."

"And why not?" Fay lifted her face. She looked at him almost defiantly. "You know that Philip promised me . . . "

"Hilary's here now. You can't leave her."

Two bright flags of colour burned in Fay's cheeks. "And why not? You left me when I'd only been out here two weeks."

Dan's mouth was a thin line. "That was different," he said, clipping his words. "We had to have some money. You know why. We've been over this a thousand times before."

"If you could leave me here, why can't we leave Hilary . . . " Fay almost shouted at him, her eyes blazing.

Hilary moved uneasily. "I'm sure I'll be all right, Dan," she said placatingly, not quite sure what they were arguing about.

Dan glanced at her, his eyes like slate. "You couldn't be left."

Fay was on her feet, hands clenched on the table. "Why not? Why not — if I could be left?"

"Because Hilary is different," he said flatly. "She's not hard . . . "

"I like that . . . " Fay screamed at him. "So I'm hard — just because I didn't make a fuss and tell everyone I was scared stiff of everything that moves, you say I'm hard . . . "

"Please . . . please . . . " Hilary said but no one was listening.

"So that's all the thanks I get . . . " Fay said, and her voice thickened. "After

87

all the things I've put up with . . . "
She rushed from the room, slamming the door behind her. The whole place seemed to rattle with the violence of it.

"Oh, Dan, you shouldn't have quarrelled over me. I'm sure I can do anything Fay can do," Hilary said miserably.

He looked at her and his voice was gentle. "Look, Hilary, I meant to say 'tough' and not 'hard'. You and Effie are completely different. You're the imaginative type; you'd die a million deaths before danger was even a mile away from you. Effie is scared of nothing for she has no imagination at all. I think that is one of our biggest problems." He sighed. "Look, do you honestly think you could live and sleep here all alone for ten days, perhaps a fortnight? I think it is asking far too much of you."

She stared at him, trying to hide the dismay that filled her. Stay here — all alone? And yet if she said that she could not do it, Fay would not be able to go. Fay would never forgive her, would resent her more than ever.

"I'd have Samson," she said, in a voice that sounded to her distressingly small.

Dan grinned. "You'd also have Petrus whom I'd trust with my life but it's the thinking, the waiting for something to happen that would get you, I'm afraid. I'd not like you to have a nervous breakdown . . . "

"Oh Dan." Thankfully, she could laugh at the very idea. "I'm sure I'd be all right," she said, more optimistically. "I'd have Samson and Petrus . . . "

"We'll talk about it later," he said gruffly and walked out.

She listened to the sound of the Rover roaring off down the hill. She stood up slowly and went to the door. It was suddenly very quiet. A quietness that you could feel. She looked over the distant valley and saw that there was not even a house to be seen. And then the telephone bell pealed. Automatically she counted the peals, as Fay had taught her. One, two, three, four long ones and one short. That was not for them. The telephone was on a party line; their call was three short rings. But she would have the telephone; in three minutes she could be in touch with someone. She would not be alone. How could she be afraid?

She went in search of Fay to tell her. Fay, stretched out on her bed, yawned, but did not deceive her sister.

"I don't care if I go or not," Fay said. "It's just that Dan's so unfair."

"But of course, you can go," Hilary said firmly. "I'll be all right, quite all right by myself."

5

DAN was still unhappy about it, but when he saw that the more he insisted that Hilary should not be left, the more distressed she became, he finally gave way.

"You must learn to shoot," he said firmly.

"But why?" Hilary recoiled from the very thought.

Fay looked amused. "She'd be too scared to shoot anything and in any case, so long as she doesn't wander out after dark she'll be all right."

Hilary's mouth was dry but Dan looked stern. "I won't leave you unless you can shoot."

"But why?"

He gave her his special grin. "Just 'in case', Hilary. I'll feel happier about you."

Surprisingly, she proved an apt pupil. Dan was a good teacher, he was patient but very firm, and taught her how to clean the gun as well as to load it quickly. He spent hours making her shoot at broken bottles and then at moving pieces of paper. He gave her full marks for the result.

"You're a born shot," he said delightedly.

"You're a born teacher," she told him.

Fay looked bored. "When this mutual flattering session is over, perhaps you'll get us a drink, Dan."

Dan grinned at her. "You're just jealous, my girl. I thought you were a damned good shot but you'll have to look to your laurels."

Fay looked scornful. "Can you see Hilary shooting a leopard as I did — wounded and leaping at me?"

"Yes, I can," Dan said surprisingly, "Hilary isn't the coward she thinks she is. She has plenty of courage — it's just the anticipation that gets her."

"Oh, Dan, I think I'd faint," Hilary said.

Fay looked pleased. "Yes, I think you would, too. However, it's quite an idea to be handy with a gun. You never know when a snake might pitch up — "

Hilary shuddered. "I think I'd die . . . "

Dan looked at her and frowned. "I wish you'd snap out of this habit of always running yourself down, Hilary."

Fay yawned mightily. "What about that drink, Dan?"

"All you think of," he grumbled but moved obediently towards the drink cupboard. "Your usual cold drink, Hilary?"

She took a deep breath. "No, I think I'd like a gin and lime this time, Dan."

He looked at her and grinned. "It's not necessary to drink to prove yourself."

"Stop fussing," Fay said irritably. "It's time Hilary grew up."

Hilary kept the smile on her face but it felt stiff. The atmosphere seemed to grow worse instead of better. Even Dan's quick defence of her made things worse, for now Fay seemed to think they were what she called 'ganging up' on her. And Fay in a difficult mood was quite impossible. It would be a relief when they went — at least, then there would be no bickering.

★ ★ ★

And then the safari was only a day or two away, and Fay changed completely. She was excited about her forthcoming trip, as she paraded for Hilary in her crisp khaki slacks and shirt with the large sun hat perched at a provocative angle on her head. Hilary was a little surprised but as Fay explained what the trip meant to her, she began to understand a little better.

"We find that when there is a husband and wife going on safari, they like to go with a couple so that the evenings aren't boring," Fay laughed gaily. "Just think — sitting in the jungle and surrounded by every kind of wild beast — we spend our evenings drinking and playing bridge."

"But isn't it very difficult — I mean, in a tent?" Hilary asked.

Fay soon enlightened her. "We travel in luxury. Philip's company organises everything but we take along the whole works, even to a portable refrigerator. We cart fresh fruit and vegetables, tins of fruit, water filters." Again she laughed. "It's far more luxurious than my normal life. We have a dining tent with a mosquito netting so that the sides can be rolled up and we dine in the open air and yet are safe from mosquitos and things. We have servants to wait on us hand and foot, plenty to drink and eat. It's a wonderful life, Hilary. During the day everything is exciting — you never know what animal you are going to hunt. Then there is usually the thrill of being in danger — though Dan takes care of that side of it very adequately and nothing can really harm us unless we are very silly — and at night we shower and change into something pretty and sit round and talk. Oh, I assure you we are very sophisticated." Again that happy laugh.

"Isn't it awkward if you don't like them?"

Fay looked shocked. "But my dear, of course we like them. It's our job to like them. Some of the women are awful drips but most of the men are very amusing. I get some lovely presents sometimes."

★ ★ ★

And then quite suddenly, the great day arrived. Hilary awoke at the first sign of dawn to hear Fay humming under her breath and to smell the fragrance of coffee. She slipped on her dressing-gown and went to join them. Fay was so excited that she could not keep still. Dan was stolid and very earnest; checking the final details, giving curt orders to Petrus, turning for a last worried look at Hilary.

"Don't forget the telephone, Hilary. You can get through to Philip if you are worried at all. I wish . . . I hope . . . " he hesitated. "I hope you'll be all right."

"Oh, Dan," Fay said impatiently, "do stop flapping. Anyone would think Hilary was a child the way you go on. You'll put the wind up her if you keep fussing so. You know Petrus is to be trusted and nothing can happen." She looked at her watch. "We ought to get cracking."

As she bent to kiss Hilary, she gave her a warm impulsive hug. "We must fix a safari for you, darling, you'd be thrilled."

"Have fun — " Hilary said.

Her last glimpse of Fay was as the tall girl turned in the doorway, her face bright and warm. "Oh, I will, darling, trust me."

Hilary went out on the *stoep* to watch the clouds of dust as the Rover sped down the track. They were joining the Americans at Monsimbe. It seemed very quiet after the last of the dust had fallen. Samson came to prowl and lean against her. She looked at the clock just four-thirty. She gave a big yawn and went back to bed, hearing Carl begin his low off-key chant as he started to clean the lounge.

Petrus awoke her with a tray of tea. He beamed and said: "Gooder-morning."

Dan had told her that Petrus spoke some English but was too lazy to do so while Fay — with her very adequate command of several African languages was around. Dan had also written out a list of phrases for her so that she could say when she wanted tea made, or the fire lighted, or for instructions for Simon in the garden. Now she swiftly washed in the hot water waiting her, dressed in a thin shantung frock and went for her breakfast, Samson close at her heels.

How quiet and peaceful it was as she ate the fried bacon and egg and drank Petrus's strong coffee. The quietness seemed to penetrate the little house and was comforting. She relaxed afterwards in a chair, her hands folded, and gazed around her. She had not realized how much Fay's restlessness and discontentment had affected her, nor how the bickering had exhausted her, until this moment when she was alone.

The morning drifted by pleasantly. After lunch she dozed, Samson stretched out on the floor by her side. She awakened and had tea on the *stoep*, gazing over the distant plain, searching through Dan's binoculars for the wild game that everyone but herself could see. She found it hard to believe that she was in Africa. The life here was absurdly similar to life in a country village except that here you were a prisoner, unable to walk out because of the risk of snakes, with no friendly villagers to chat to, or little homely post office to visit. Yet she did not feel lonely. The quietness was so restful . . .

Her first bad moment came when she sat in the lounge, waiting for Petrus to bring in the lamps. The African twilight descended without warning and one moment, it was daylight and the next, quite dark. She sat on, feeling the dark shadows in the room stretching out towards her, feeling chilly, desolate, a little uneasy. Luckily Samson snorted in his sleep and began to cry softly, twitching in his dream, and it dispelled the ominous moment.

Hilary stood and walked through her bedroom and the pantry. The back door was open and she shouted: "Petrus — Petrus — the lamps."

Petrus came running — the thin Carl close behind.

"Sorry — sorry — Madame . . . " Petrus kept saying. Soon the two lamps were being pumped, the little room bright with light, the frightening shadows pushed away. Then Petrus came running with iced water and Hilary, feeling a little self-conscious, poured herself out a very mild drink. She switched on the radio and sat listening to records of dance music and Samson came to put his great head in her lap and gaze up at her.

Dinner was served punctually and was the usual Tommy meat with tinned vegetables. Coffee came, hot and strong, and then the sounds of Petrus in the kitchen and his loud voice and Carl's as they joked and laughed. It seemed to her they were making more noise than usual; and she wondered uneasily if she should tell them to be quiet. Were they taking advantage of her, she wondered. Fay said you had to be stern with the *boys* or they did not respect you. But it was not easy to be stern when you could not speak the language.

There was a good play on the radio and Hilary listened with enjoyment. It was quite a shock to look at the clock and see it was nearly ten. She stood up and yawned lazily — went out on to the *stoep*, Samson by her side.

The quietness was intense. As she stood there, gazing across the plain, she could not see a light anywhere. The silvery moon was cold and etched deep shadows where the hillside fell away. There was silence from the *boys'* quarters and she was suddenly aware of her complete isolation.

Giving a shiver, she turned indoors and bolted the front door. She went through the bedrooms and to the pantry and locked the back door. Samson, close at heel, she mocked herself as she carried the lamp and peered under the beds and into the cupboard but, all the same, she felt much happier when she knew everything was locked. Samson sprawled on the rug in the larger bedroom and Hilary, not feeling inclined for bed, went back to her armchair. The radio was switched low and she began to read an English magazine. She did not know how long she had been reading when she heard a sound —

Lowering the book she listened. Someone was scratching at the front door. She sat very still but she felt as if the blood had drained out of her body. She could not breathe for a moment. At the same moment there was a sudden gust of wind through the room and the lamps flickered, the bright light of the lamps fading and almost vanishing and then flaring up again, so that one smoked and she had to move hastily to adjust the wick. The scratching at the door came again.

She stood, leaning against the table, her hand to her mouth as she waited.

And then Samson barked.

She swung round. The bark had not come from the bedroom. It was outside. She managed to move towards the bedroom, to push open the door. Samson was not there — and the window over the bed was wide open. He must have jumped up while she was reading and pushed it open.

She went to the front door and opened it. Samson stood there, wagging his tail delightedly, leaping up at her. Feeling sick with relief and ashamed of her panic, she let him in and bolted the door again, taking him with her to the bedroom and this time, making sure the window was locked.

The telephone bell rang sharply. Without thought, she answered it. A woman was speaking:

" — and I said to her — " The voice snapped off abruptly. And then the woman spoke again, in an angry annoyed voice. "I do declare, darling, someone is listening in again on this line. You'd think people would have more decency than to horn in on private conversations . . . "

Her cheeks bright red, Hilary replaced the receiver carefully. She stood there, feeling she had been caught out in some crime. Yet she had not intended to listen in — it was just that she had forgotten it was a party line.

The voice helped her, though She realized that she was not so far from civilization after all. In a moment, she could speak to another human being on the telephone. If she was in trouble, she could ask for help.

It helped her to undress and get into bed. She shut the doors of the room and had Samson sleeping on the rug by her side. She closed her eyes because the darkness seemed to press against her. She began to wish she had not turned out both the lamps. But she had a torch, and the moonlight, in any case, poured in through the small barred window. It was hot and stuffy in the room yet she did not feel she would be happy with the window open — or even the door.

It was a long time before she dozed and then she awoke, trembling. Somewhere an animal was making a terrible noise coughing. Was it a lion, prowling round outside?

She sat up in bed. Samson blissfully snored. Reassured, Hilary lay down again and tried to sleep. There was another choking noise — it sounded outside the window. She lay there, pulling the sheet up to her chin, waiting . . . waiting . . .

When she awoke, Petrus was standing by the bed, the sun streaming in through the window, as he put the tea tray on the table by her side. She lay there and stared at him stupidly.

"Morning, 'Nkosikas . . . " he said politely and tiptoed out of the room.

She began to laugh — the laughter got a bit mixed up with tears, but the hot tea made her feel better. What was the good of locking every door in the house? Petrus could find a way in — and if he could, so could anyone who wanted to.

She had a bath in the hip-bath, Petrus bringing buckets of boiling water and filling it for her first. Lying back, soaking in the warm water she saw a small red thing stuck in her skin.

A tick!

The most absurd panic flooded her

— she felt sick and disgusted but she remembered that Dan had told her to remove a tick carefully, making sure you did not leave the head behind in the skin, as a very septic sore might result.

It took a lot of courage to grasp the tick firmly, to ease it out of her skin. She flung it away with a shudder and hastily dried herself. She wished with all her heart that she had never left England — that she could catch the next plane home, back to the quiet safe life she knew and loved.

But she felt better when she went out into the garden. She was filled with a new energy and as she wandered round Dan's rather pathetic garden she decided that she would tackle it. She called Simon, who was dozing in a corner by the tools and showed him what she wanted dug up. She ignored his pained look and watched his slow movements impatiently, seizing the spade herself and showing him how to do it. The perspiration poured off her but it seemed to release something inside her. She began to weed vigorously, keeping near him, telling him sharply to get on with the digging.

Samson came to watch, looked shocked and drifted off to a shady corner. Hilary worked on, feeling the sun gaze down and her thin dress stick to her wet skin, but there was a comforting satisfaction in the labour. Dan was fond of gardening but he said it was discouraging, unless you watched the garden *boy* strictly, he would pull out flowering strawberries blandly or dig out precious bulbs just as they sprouted. Well, she had all the time in the world and would keep an eye on the boy. She began to plan as she worked, her small but strong hands clutching the weeds firmly, wrestling with long roots. She called Simon to help her when they proved too strong. She wondered if she could make Petrus understand if she told him to drive her to Monsimbe in the old car. She would find shops that sold seeds there.

Petrus came to tell her tea was ready. She sat on the *stoep*, drinking it and feeling pleasantly exhausted. He came to ask her what she would eat for lunch. Fay had shown her the stack of tinned foods and had given her the key to the store cupboard. Now Hilary and

Petrus discussed meals for the day and she weighed out sugar and mealie meal as Fay had instructed her.

She was reading her book, deciding she would not garden until late afternoon, when Petrus came to her.

"Very — sick — very sick, indeed," he said gravely. "You come right away."

She could not make out what he meant but he kept pointing to the house so she followed him. In the lounge was a white overall which he held for her to put on. He led the way to the pantry. There on the ground outside the kitchen door, lay a tall thin African. His hair was grizzled. There was a deep wound in his head, and the blood had congealed, with flies swarming on it.

"'Nkosikas make well," Petrus directed. Carl came with a bowl of water and a bottle of disinfectant, a box of bandages, and book of first-aid. Both waited, looking at her expectantly.

Hilary hesitated. Fay had once said jokingly that there had not been so many broken crowns lately but that at any moment, one would turn up. Hilary had paid little attention, thinking that anyone hurt would go to hospital, not realizing that in this land of great distances, first-aid had to be given on the spot and by amateurs.

She had no choice when they looked at her so trustingly; so — trying not to feel nauseated by the stench that came from the African on the ground — Hilary forced herself to bathe the deep wound. She was afraid of starting a fresh haemorrhage but as she washed away the dried blood, she saw that the wound was already healing of its own accord.

"'Nkosikas want needle?" Petrus asked.

Hilary suppressed a shudder. "No," she said grimly. She looked at the wound. It seemed healthy enough. She found on the tray Carl was holding for her some acriflavine emulsion and decided to use that. Soon the broken head was bound up and Petrus and Carl were beaming at her with delight.

"'Nkosikas very good medicine," Petrus said slowly.

Hilary went to the bathroom, Petrus close at hand with hot water. She scrubbed her hands carefully and was relieved, when she came out of the hut, to see her patient had been removed. She went back to her chair on the *stoep* and proceeded to study the first-aid book.

As a Girl Guide, she had enjoyed the first-aid classes but that seemed years ago. Now she felt horribly inadequate and a little scared of what else she might be asked to do, now that she had 'proved' herself.

It was in the middle of the afternoon, as she lay dozing on her bed that she heard the car. She jumped up quickly, slipping on her dress, running a comb through her hair, and went out to the *stoep*, eagerly.

A green Rover stopped. A tall man with dark hair and cold grey eyes got out and came towards her. Philip Randel. And in a tearing temper.

He stared at the slight girl and wondered what on earth had happened to her. She had always looked frail but now her eyes were like great saucers in her thin pointed face.

"So it's true?" he demanded angrily.

"What's true?"

He came to tower over her, looking even taller than usual in his khaki shorts and bush jacket. "Have they left you here alone?" he demanded. "Did Fenella — your sister, go with her husband?"

"Yes." Hilary took a deep breath. "Yes, she has gone with Dan," she said defiantly.

"Just wait until I see Dan!" Philip exploded.

"Look — it was my idea. Dan didn't want to go . . . " Hilary began hastily as she remembered that Fay had said Philip could cause Dan to lose his job.

Philip looked disbelieving. "I suppose Dan was afraid of offending the Latchmeres . . . "

Hilary took another deep breath and sought wildly for the right words. If she let Dan get the blame, he might get into trouble. But were she to tell the truth — that Fay had practically insisted on going and had behaved so that Hilary had no choice but to say she would be all right alone — then Philip Randel would not believe her.

"It was my own idea to stay here," she said, furious with Fay for placing her in such a position; furious with Philip for his anger; furious with herself because Philip

110

always made her feel as if she had been hauled up before an angry headmistress. "I'm quite all right here."

He calmed down and looked at her. "Have you been ill?"

"M'm. I had dysentery and colic."

He frowned. "Seen a doctor? Fenella — I mean, Fay didn't tell me."

So Fay HAD seen him, Hilary thought quickly. On one of her trips alone to Monsimbe, of course.

"I'm all right, now. Fay says everyone gets it at first."

He was suddenly aware that she was looking very white and that the sun was blazing down on them.

"May I come in for a moment?"

"Of course. Will you have some tea or a drink?"

He looked at her sharply. "Caught the habit already?"

She felt her cheeks burn. "I mean an iced soft drink, of course."

"I'd prefer tea," he said, just to be difficult.

He sat down while she went to call Petrus. When she returned they sat in awkward silence, both aware that there were things that should be discussed between them.

Tea was a welcome interruption. After his second cup, Philip looked at her grimly. "Don't tell me you didn't die a million different deaths here alone last night."

She stared at him. Why must he always take such a domineering, unpleasant tone when he spoke to her? She was angry with him because he was concerned about her. Suddenly the humour of the situation struck her. How inconsistent could one be?

"Yes, I was scared," she admitted, and told him the whole story. "You've no idea what a fool I felt when I realized that no matter how well I locked up, nothing stayed locked. It was silly to be afraid, I realize that, but there are such strange sounds at night and . . ."

"I don't think it's silly. You'd be a strange person if you weren't scared," he said crisply. "Look, I'll send over my police *boy* every night to keep an eye on things. I can trust him implicitly and he'll walk round all the time. In any case, Hilary," he smiled at her, and for a moment it was the Philip Randel she had liked so much on the plane, "you're safe up here. It's too exposed for animals to get near and there's nothing to attract them. No chickens or cattle. Remember how far sound travels on a quiet night — the lion you heard coughing was probably miles away."

He stood up to go. "You're sure you wouldn't rather I ran you into Monsimbe? You could stay at the hotel there for the ten days your sister is away," he suggested.

She was tempted to accept. But the next minute, she knew she could not give way to such weakness. It would prove for ever what a coward she was. After all, if Fay could live in this house alone it should be possible for her to do so, too.

"Thank you," she smiled up at him. "I'll be quite all right. All the same," she temporized, "I'll be very grateful for your police boy."

She walked with him to his Rover. He hesitated, looking down at her.

"I'll give you a ring tomorrow. I'd like to take you to meet a few of the people who live round here."

"Thank you," she said politely. "You are very kind."

He drove off still worrying about her but not quite sure what else he could do. He felt fresh anger with Dan — the man ought to know better than to go off and leave a raw girl alone. The job was not as important as all that. He could have arranged for another couple to take the Americans.

6

PHILIP telephoned her the following morning. She had just come in from the garden, Samson snuffling affectionately at her heels, when she heard the bell ring. It took a little while before she realized that it was their number being rung. She had not thought of anyone telephoning her.

He sounded quite concerned. "Was it better last night?"

"Much, much better," she lied, and hoped it was convincing. It would be ungrateful to confess that the regular flashing of the police guard's torch on the ceiling every time he passed the window, had been almost as disturbing as the lion's roar. "Your police *boy* reported to me. How smart he is, Philip; I felt much happier with him around." It would be childish to say that Samson's soft menacing growl every time he heard the policeman's footsteps — the tall African in his smart khaki had worn shiny brown

115

boots — had kept jerking her awake.

"I'm glad," Philip said crisply. "I was rather worried about you but I was sure you'd feel better with Absalom around. Now, I propose to pick you up soon after four. It will take us about an hour to get to the Hendriks. We're going there to a cocktail-party to welcome a new D.C. Are you one of those people who have no idea of time, like Fen — like your sister; or can I rely on you to be ready?"

"I'll be ready, of course." Already with a few sentences, he had begun to antagonize her.

"Wear that pretty frock you wore at the dance," he commanded. "Good-bye." He rang off.

She replaced the receiver slowly — and suddenly wondered how many listening ears there had been on the party line. Maybe that was why Philip was so curt.

The day dragged a little. She felt heavy with lack of sleep and after lunch, she lay on her bed, dozing. She awoke with a shock and saw that she had less than half an hour in which to dress. That meant no bath — but she would have a cold shower.

Twenty minutes later, already getting sticky again from the heat despite the temporary coldness from the shower, she was brushing her hair with vigorous movements, twisting the curling ends round her fingers, wishing she had hair like Fay's. She was not sure if she was thrilled at the idea of the cocktail-party or scared. Fay had once said that there were a lot of *cats* in the neighbourhood; that in such a small community, scandal was all you had to talk about, and that if you did nothing worth talking about, someone was sure to invent something.

She was waiting on the *stoep* when Philip arrived. His eyes approved what they saw when he looked at her. She had on her finest nylons, her evening shoes with the spidery heels, the green necklace and ear-rings her mother had given her for Christmas and, of course, the coral-red frock.

Samson watched them rather mournfully but Hilary soon forgot him as the Rover lurched forward and then stopped. Philip looked at her.

"You'll want a coat."

"But the evenings are so hot and we

shan't be very late."

He looked amused. "Won't we? These cocktail-parties often go on all night. Get a coat, there's a good girl, I promise you it can be very cold around 1 a.m."

One a.m., she thought! Some cocktail-party. She began to wish she had had something to eat for tea. Lurching down the winding hill, Philip stared straight ahead. The girl still didn't look well. No doubt a thing such as had happened to her was a terrific mental shock. His hands gripped the steering wheel as he thought of the man who had let this kid down. Fenella had told him the whole story. How Hilary had been in love with a man fifteen years older than herself; how their parents had disapproved, had stipulated a year's engagement, how — at the end of the year — they had reluctantly given their consent, only to have the man walk out on Hilary a few days before the wedding.

"That is why she made up that fantastic story about coming to look after my mythical children," Fenella had said, half-laughing, yet with affection in her voice. "Poor little Hilary. She thought the man was wonderful and after sticking to him and almost defying the parents she found he didn't want her. You can guess how humiliated she felt. Mother thought this was the best solution and, of course it is. But it will take time. Hilary hasn't even mentioned it to me. Maybe she thinks I know nothing about it; Mother would very probably let her believe that no one knows. Just at the moment," she had gone on when he suggested that she introduce Hilary to the neighbourhood, "she is so very sensitive, she can't bear to meet anyone. Just give her time, Philip," Fenella had finished, her bright blue eyes appealing, her hand resting lightly on his.

But now he felt that Fenella was wrong. Although quite obviously the child was very embarrassed about the lies she had told, he felt that she needed to meet people, to have to face facts. After all, life wasn't over at twenty just because one man has let you down.

He began to tell her something of the people she would meet.

"There's Mrs. Adams. She's in her sixties and quite a person, or at least, she thinks so. She and the other women fight terribly. She thinks she is always right and they resent it — particularly as she usually is." He chuckled.

It startled Hilary for he so rarely laughed. Now, glancing at him, she saw that he was in a good mood. Unconsciously she relaxed and some of the tension left her.

"Mrs. Adams has had a sad story, Hilary," he went on, frowning a little as he concentrated on driving down a particularly steep decline. "They were in a very good position in India and then when India and Pakistan became independent, the Adams, like so many other old Indian Army folk, were redundant. John Adams was too set in his ways to start all over again but he managed, through influence, to get a job here as Public Relations Officer to a big firm. He does his job adequately but that is all. They still miss India and all it meant to them, particularly as they lost two sons there during a rising. She's difficult to please and has high standards, but when she hears who your father is, I'm sure she'll welcome you."

"Are there many young people?" Hilary ventured to ask. Usually with Philip these days, she sat back and listened.

He told her there were. There were the Foss's, husband and wife, both in late twenties. "They're like Dan and Fen — your sister; both work for me on safari trips. A nice couple but . . . " he hesitated for a moment, "don't believe all either of them tell you. They like to scare newcomers. Seem to find it funny." He spoke with a bitterness that surprised her. "They have no imagination," he added.

"Then there's Anna Wendel — " his voice changed again. "She's a nice unassuming pleasant little thing and recently got married to one of our most dashing hunters," he said sarcastically. "Everyone is surprised but she seems to be making him happy."

Listening as he told her of other young couples, of the new D.C. and the wife he had just brought back from England and who was a famous model, Hilary wondered what people were going to say about her.

They drove for nearly an hour through

a sandy plain, with here and there thorn trees, and occasionally an umbrella tree. It was not very green, for the rains had not arrived yet; and it was very hot. The cloud of dust they were throwing up behind them also seemed to seep inside the Rover and she began to feel sticky and uncomfortable. It was a relief when the Rover started climbing, twisting and turning as the road wound round a narrow rocky *koppie*. The house was visible a long time before they reached it. It was a big house, painted white, with round pillars holding up the roof on the veranda. Cars of every shape and size — but all dusty — were parked in the drive, and Hilary was very glad of Philip's warm hand under her elbow as they climbed the steps, for her courage was disappearing.

Inside the house, they were surrounded by people. Hilary felt dazed and her face began to ache with smiling as she was introduced by Philip first to one person and then another. Everyone smiled at her but she sensed judgment in their cool eyes and she began to wish Philip had never suggested this visit.

Slowly people began to become personalities. She saw what a formidable person Mrs. Adams was, with her pouter bosom tightly encased in grey silk, and her lorgnette which she used only when she wanted to make some crushing remark. She was gentle with Hilary and had heard of her father so they had plenty to talk about. One remark she made disturbed Hilary, but there was no time to puzzle it out.

"I can't believe it, my dear child. When I heard that you had been left alone, I rang Philip instantly and demanded that something be done about you. I found he knew nothing about it. How could your sister have left you there alone? Especially at this time, my dear child, when you should not be left alone with your thoughts. I can understand how she could do it — but why did you let her? You've character in that face of yours even if you do look too scared to say boo to a goose."

"I'm quite all right alone."

"M'm," Mrs. Adams grunted. "At least, you've got pluck."

Several people said strange things.

They all seemed sorry for her and yet trying to hide it. Hilary liked the Hendriks, who were giving the party. In their forties, both lean and tough as leather, they lived there because they loved it.

"You see, part of our farm is on the boundaries of the game reserve. That means we see animals all the time. I take photos and my wife records their cries," Joel Hendrik told her as he refilled her glass with sherry. "It's fascinating. I've got a wonderful photograph of a python swallowing a young buck." Hilary shivered and saw his eyes glint with amusement. "This is nature in the raw, you know," he told her.

Jennifer Hendriks chimed in, her arm lightly round Hilary: "You don't need to tell this child that. I think you're very brave to stay there alone. Aren't you scared?"

Hilary smiled. "Sometimes."

"Of course you are. I'm used to it now but it's all new to you. Where do you come from? London or the depths of the country."

"Somerset — just a village near Pill."

"Lovely country . . . "

The new D.C. was introduced, a short tubby man with a dark moustache and beard and very long slim hands. He beamed at Hilary.

"You and Rhoda must get together. Where is she . . . " He looked round and a tall slim girl came towards them. Her oval face was pale, her eyes very dark and heavily made-up, her hair curled slightly round her head. She moved beautifully — you could see what an excellent model she must have been.

Now she smiled at Hilary. "Hullo, greenhorn," she said. "At least we are both dark so we can't be called *rooineks*." She laughed at Hilary's bemused expression. "That's Afrikaans for red-necks. Most English people get very burnt in the sun."

Hilary flushed. It seemed to her that Rhoda was mocking her, speaking as though to a child.

"I hear you have a very attractive sister," Rhoda went on. "I'm looking forward to meeting her." Her eyes danced maliciously. She bent closer and said: "My dear, have you ever seen anyone funnier than Ma Adams? She thinks she knows everything and that we all owe her allegiance. This ghastly Empire business, don't you know," she lifted her hand as if holding a lorgnette and gazed severely at Hilary.

Hilary flushed again, uncomfortable and afraid Mrs. Adams might have seen. She was glad when the languid Rhoda moved on and a short slight girl came to smile shyly at Hilary.

"I'm Anna Wendel," she introduced herself. "We were all so excited when we heard you'd arrived. There are so few people here, that it is lovely to have visitors."

They sat side by side chatting and it was over half an hour before a movement of Anna's head gave Hilary the chance to see that the girl had a purple birthmark running down the side of her face. Hilary caught her breath and tried to behave as if she had not noticed it but Anna would not let her.

She smiled at Hilary. "So you've seen it? Sometimes I'm foolish enough to try to hide it from newcomers. Most people here don't notice it any more and I've had it all my life so I ought not to mind."

"It's not very noticeable," Hilary lied, but Anna smiled.

"You're sweet, but it is. However, Burt doesn't mind it so why should I?"

"Burt? That is your husband, isn't it?" Hilary asked, remembering what Philip had said in the Rover.

"Yes." Anna pointed out a tall man on the other side of the room. "That's my husband," she said simply. Looking at her, Hilary saw the rather ordinary face suddenly glowing. The man across the room, as if he sensed that they were talking about him, looked over the heads of the people between and waved.

He was very handsome, Hilary thought, if that was the type you found handsome. As he made his way slowly towards them, he had a swashbuckling air. He looked as if he should have been a pirate or smuggler. His features were very regular with a cleft in the chin and a wicked gleam in his eyes. He was tall and very broad-shouldered and he walked with a sort of swagger.

As he reached them he smiled at his

wife and Hilary felt a cold shiver slide down her back. Anna might be plain, even, by some people's ideas, disfigured, but this man loved her very much. He took Hilary's hand and held it lightly, smiling down at her.

"So this is the poor little sister. You don't look very sad . . . " he began.

Anna cried out — she had knocked her glass off the small table.

"Darling . . . " he scolded gently and took out his handkerchief, mopping up the mess. "What will Hilary think of you? That you imbibe too much?"

Anna laughed. She looked triumphant rather than upset by her accident.

"She can see I'm drinking tomato juice so she won't be so foolish."

Burt studied Hilary and she saw in his expression that he was used to being admired and even chased by women. Perhaps that was why he loved quiet little Anna. "You're not like your sister at all," he said almost accusingly.

Hilary smiled. "Everyone says that."

"Same parents? Not one father and a different mother sort of thing?"

Hilary shook her head. "Same parents.

They've been married thirty years."

He whistled and looked at his wife. "Lucky people," he said softly and turned away.

It was midnight before the party ended. Snacks had been served and then at ten, bowls of iced soup had come round followed by water-thin sandwiches of chicken and tomato. Hilary's head ached and her eyes burned from the smoky room but as she sat by Philip's side in the Rover, she felt more contented than she had since she arrived.

"Enjoy yourself?" he asked once.

"Oh, yes," she gasped, clinging to the guard rail before her as they bucked and rocketed over the road. "Very much, thank you. I thought they were all very nice."

"Were the Foss's very unpleasant?"

She tried to remember the young cynical couple who had teased her about not being taken on safari with her sister.

"No," she said very thoughtfully. "But . . . but I got the impression that they didn't like Fay very much."

The Rover shot forward suddenly as

though he had stepped on the accelerator. "Of course they don't. Dan and Fenella — your sister — are a much better pair of hunters. Tallulah hates roughing it and Ned drinks too much. They're jealous, that's all." She was silent for so long that he turned to look at her. "Now what's worrying you?"

"Nothing," she said slowly. "But — but there seems so much rivalry and . . . what you call jealousy. Is it necessary? I mean, can't they just take it in turns."

Philip's shout of laughter made her jump. "You are so young," he said scornfully. "Don't you see that it's just that spirit of rivalry that keeps them all on their toes. There has to be rivalry and competition in the world."

"I think it's a pity," she said flatly.

When they reached home, Philip went all through the little house with a powerful torch, Samson sniffing suspiciously at his heels. The African police guard came up and saluted smartly. Philip spoke to him and then said good night to Hilary.

"You coming to church on Sunday?"

Stifling a yawn, she stared at him. "Is

there a church here?"

"They're building one in Monsimbe but at the moment, we take it in turns to hold it in our homes. Next Sunday it's being held at my house. Would you like to come? Our padre is quite a human bloke. Actually we were in the war together."

"How would I get there?"

"I'll send for you. See you on Sunday then. Good night."

It seemed very quiet after he had gone but as she lay in bed, listening to rustles and queer noises from outside, she felt sleep creeping upon her. She lay smiling, thinking how nice some people were and looking forward to seeing them again. This might be what Fay called the 'bundu' but there were people willing to be friendly after all. But just at the last moment, she thought of something that had worried her. The questions asked as to how well she knew Philip — the sly insinuations that they were sorry for her — and the hostility she had sensed towards Fay. Were they even now discussing *her*, Hilary wondered, and if so, what were they saying? Philip had dismissed the hostility lightly, calling it 'jealousy', but she had sensed the hostility in the men's voices, too. Particularly in that nice Anna's husband — the very good-looking one who looked such a swash-buckler. Hilary would have thought he and Fay would have liked one another — they both had a driving vitality that could not be missed. She sighed deeply and turned over, tucking her hands under her cheek. It had been a pleasant evening and Africa quite suddenly, seemed a very much nicer place.

7

HILARY's first glimpse of Philip's home made her catch her breath with delight. It was built on a flat plateau of stone on the side of a mountain. The view was difficult to see that first day because the unusual heat haze obscured everything — but she could see enough to make her realize what it must be like on a fine clear day. They were two thousand feet above the valley and the air seemed crisper and less sticky. Far, far below them, Hilary could see smaller *koppies* sticking up like children's sandcastles. Some of them were thickly forested, others as bare as the rock they were made of.

Hilary's police *boy* had fetched her in the Rover and as she got out of it, she felt very self-conscious. There was no garden round the house; it was all paving stones, with huge tubs of flowering shrubs everywhere. She could hear laughter and chatter from the house and on one side could see several cars parked. She had dressed carefully, thinking that perhaps out here they treated it as an English Sunday, and when Philip came down the two granite steps that led to the long L-shaped timber house, she was glad that she was wearing a hat and white gloves to go with her white shoes and pale green shantung frock, because, in the doorway, she could see several women standing, each one wearing a hat.

"Hullo." Philip smiled at her and took her hand.

"I hope I'm not late. We drove very fast."

"That Absalom," Philip frowned, "I told him to drive very carefully."

"I wasn't scared," she assured him quickly, "and I thought him a very good driver." She was always desperately worried lest she unwittingly get another person into trouble. She had no idea how she looked to those inside the house, who were even now turning curious eyes towards them.

So small and thin with that peaky little face and enormous eyes, the dark curly hair with the sober little white hat set solemnly and straightly on top of it; with her eager placating face turned up to Philip's.

"I won't sack him," he said quickly and with a smile, "so don't worry."

"Oh, I'm so glad. I feel much safer with him. He walks round all night long."

"He'd better," Philip said grimly, and took her arm as they went into the house. "Welcome to Stonehenge."

She caught herself starting to giggle. "Is that really its name?"

He looked down at her soberly. "What's wrong with it?"

"Oh, Philip, but it's nothing like . . . "

He grinned at that. "Well, what shall I call it? Cosinook? Cuminside? Restcote?"

She could not help laughing. "Oh, Philip . . . "

So they came into the group, holding hands and laughing at a shared joke. Mrs. Adams and several others exchanged significant looks and more than one whispered to another and grinned delightedly.

It was a large and airy house. Hilary liked the cool green curtains that hung in silken folds to the floor — she liked the enormous and very comfortable chintz-covered armchairs. She liked the few, very good, oil paintings of sea scenes; great angry green waves dashing against a small ship; a slow peaceful tidal river with its curved foam-flecked scallops on the yellow sand. She liked the way the dining-room had been cleared and made into a temporary chapel — huge urns of white lilies flanking the improvised altar where candles flickered in the breeze from the open window.

The Padre proved to be a Father Brown, a tall, very thin man with yellowed cheeks and very bright keen blue eyes. He looked at her sharply and with some bewilderment as he talked to her. She did not strike him as a girl who had been publicly humiliated and whose heart must be cracked, if not broken. She talked easily of her father in England and he said that he was afraid his sermon could not compete with her father's. "Or don't you listen to sermons?" he asked with a smile. "So many people tell me they think of other things."

She looked very shocked. "Of course

I listen. It would be terribly rude not to. I know how much trouble a sermon makes, how hard they are to write."

"Thanks be, I've found one sympathizer," he smiled at her. He thought how different she was from her sister.

It was a simple service, designed to suit the tastes of several different denominations. A simple service of praise for what had been received and prayer for help in solving their troubles. Kneeling next to Philip, Hilary felt filled with a new strength. That night she would not be afraid. Nor would she let Fay's moods worry her. Indeed, when Fay returned, they would have a serious talk. Kneeling there and hearing the familiar words, Hilary knew one thing. She could not lie to her mother. She would tell Fay so and then write to her mother explaining the whole situation, and begging her not to let it affect her feelings for Fay.

She stood up, feeling much happier. Afterwards, tea and cakes were served and Hilary found herself next to Mrs. Adams.

"Well, dear, and how did you like our little party?"

"Oh, very much indeed," Hilary smiled happily at her. "I had been feeling very lonely and as if we were miles and miles from people. I did not realize people were so near."

Mrs. Adams's mouth set grimly. "It was your sister's place to introduce you to us."

A stab of dismay went through Hilary. As usual, she had said the wrong thing and got poor Fay into more trouble.

"She was going to," she said very hastily — too hastily, Mrs. Adams noticed — "but I was ill. I had dysentery and colic and had to stay in bed. Then, when I was better, she and Dan had to go on this safari . . . "

Mrs. Adams sniffed. "I see," she said, rather disagreeably. "And have you made any friends since the party?"

"Oh, yes!" Hilary leapt at the chance to change the conversation. "Anna. She drove over to see me two days after the party and had tea. I think she is so nice — so easy to talk to and . . . " Even as she spoke she was remembering how strange it had seemed to her to be told

138

by Anna that she had never been to the house before.

"But don't Fay and Dan ever entertain?" Hilary had asked.

Anna had smiled ruefully. "Oh, yes, but not us. She can't stand us."

It had made Hilary feel uncomfortable. Ought she to be entertaining Anna in Fay's house, if Fay had some legitimate reason for not wanting to ask them there? Yet what could Anna and Burt have done to offend Fay?

"Pity about Anna's face," Mrs. Adams said. "It must surely cause her to worry lest she lose that husband of hers."

Hilary was shocked and quite unable to hide it. "But they are terribly in love."

"Now," Mrs. Adams said significantly. "He was always a wild young man, caused his parents a lot of anxiety. The only thing in his favour is that he never had any use for . . . " She stopped and across her plump face, there slowly spread a crimson stain of embarrassment. "But what am I doing," Mrs. Adams hastily went on, "gossiping to a young thing like you. I should know better." She stood up and moved away to another group, still with that embarrassed look on her face.

Philip came to sit beside Hilary, offering her sandwiches, asking her if she had liked the service.

"Very much, Philip," she said earnestly. "I liked his sermon, too. I find his religion much more — more acceptable — " the words came out in a breathless rush, "than my father's religion. I think — I think one's religion should make one happy, not terrify one with threats of hell-fire and eternal damnation for one's sins."

Philip chuckled. "You want a comfortable, non-demanding religion."

Hilary coloured. "No. I don't but . . . but I think loving God should make one tolerant, not — not narrow-minded and — and always condemning people."

Philip looked at her. "You've been talking to Mrs. Adams," he guessed shrewdly and saw how right he was from her expression. He wondered just what Mrs. Adams had been saying. It was obviously nothing to do with him, though, because Hilary was quite at ease with him, something she rarely was.

He asked Hilary to wait until the others had left and then he would drive her home. They stood on the veranda saying good-bye and he was fully aware of how significant it looked. He had not planned it deliberately but now he was glad that his name and Hilary's were being associated; it would show more emphatically that his relationship with Fenella was purely a business one.

"You'll stay to lunch," he told Hilary as they went indoors. She hesitated and thought of the lonely, uninteresting, monotonous meal that would await her at home.

"Thank you."

As the dining-room was temporarily a chapel, they lunched in Philip's study, a very masculine, almost bare room with shelves of books lining the walls — a huge picture window giving a view of the mist-hidden valley, and great dark timbers in the ceiling. It was a delicious meal and when Hilary complimented him on it, Philip chuckled.

"It always riles Fenella to see how well I live as a bachelor. You women like to think you're indispensable but I guarantee that any bachelor has better attention and far better food than any married man," he said it teasingly for he liked to see the hot colour fill her pale cheeks, liked to hear her defend people. But this time she took it seriously.

"You are probably right," she said slowly. "I wonder if it applies to spinsters. I have an aunt who is single and retired, now. She has a lovely life — beautiful clothes, a lovely tidy flat; she goes to bed at whatever hour she likes; she does as she likes."

"So you advocate single blessedness." His voice was no longer teasing. He wondered if Hilary was leading up to a confession of what had happened to her — from there, it would be an easy step to admit she had invented 'Jackie' and Fenella's baby. There would be a happier friendship between them if they could sweep those lies out of the way.

Hilary ate the iced paw paw and looked at him thoughtfully. "I can imagine nothing worse," she said very slowly, "than that. I mean — " she waved her hand vaguely, "I mean, fancy growing old and having no one to worry about.

142

No one to worry about you, either. I mean, fancy having no children. Oh, no, Philip, I can't see that going through life alone is best. At least, not for a woman. It may be different for men." She looked at him inquiringly.

"It IS different for men," he said with an emphasis he had not intended. "You see . . . " he sought for the right words, "marriage, to a woman, means fulfilment, completion, the rounding off of a circle. Marriage brings her security —"

"Sometimes . . . " Hilary murmured and he looked at her with surprise.

"Usually," he said, grimly. "Security; emotional satisfaction. It satisfies her desire to mother a man, to be important with her own husband, to have her own home, and also, as you say, to have children."

"You're quite wrong," she said. "You're making out that women marry for purely selfish reasons. I don't agree. A woman marries because she wants to make the person she loves happy, to look after him, to be his companion, to have HIS children."

"Is that how you see marriage?"

143

Something in his tone made her colour again but she met his gaze. "Yes."

There was a silence as Solomon cleared the table and served coffee on the veranda. Hilary was embarrassed at the way she had spoken, she wondered if he would reopen the subject. She thought that he would not.

Surprisingly he did. "You think your sister married Dan because she wanted to make him happy?"

"Of course." Hilary stared at him. For the first time that day resentment filled her at his sarcastic tone. "She loved him terribly."

Philip frowned and stirred his coffee slowly.

"Haven't you ever been in love?" Hilary asked bravely, half-expecting him to snap at her.

It was a long moment before he lifted his head and gazed at her. "Yes."

"Then — then won't you want to make her happy?"

His eyes went back to his coffee as he considered the question. Was that his sole desire — to make her happy? To cherish her, in sickness and in health?

"I want to possess her," he said heavily.

Hilary pushed her cup and saucer away with a tiny clatter. "Then you don't love her," she said.

He looked up, quick with anger, and met her steady gaze.

"I do love her," he said. And told himself that it was the truth. She was a married woman. He had no idea if she loved him, though she swore that she did. He was not even sure that if they were free to marry, they would make a success of it, but . . . "I do love her," he said even more loudly.

Hilary stood up, shaking out her skirt and taking another glimpse at the mist-filled valley. "You don't know what love is," she said almost sadly.

"I suppose you do," he said savagely.

Again her eyes met his in a long thoughtful glance. Then she gave a little sigh. A strangely pathetic sigh. "I'm afraid I do," she told him.

Waiting for him to bring the Rover to the front door, she found she was trembling. How could a man make you feel so differently towards him;

so mixed up, so bewildered? How could you at one moment dislike the man intensely — dislike him for his domineering attitude, his cynicism, his sarcasm, and the next, tremble if he accidentally touched your hand, find your eyes searching for his in a crowded room, feel that warm glow of happiness simply because he smiled at you?

Sitting by his side, as they jerked over the road, she thought miserably that it would be better for her to go back to England.

The Rover swerved and Philip braked. He turned and grabbed a shot-gun from the back and said sharply:

"Stay where you are . . . " He slid out of the Rover and ran round to the back.

She waited, flinching, for the shot. It came. Turning her head she waited. In a moment, Philip returned and showed a very dead snake.

"My first snake," she said and shuddered.

"A Mamba," Philip said grimly. "I could have run him over but they have a nasty knack of curling up under the

Rover and later appearing. Nasty looking brute, eh?"

Hilary shivered. She waited until Philip was driving again. "It's hard," she said, "to realize that I am in Africa and surrounded by wild animals because I never see any."

He looked at her sharply. "Do you want to? Won't you be afraid?"

Her hands tightened in her lap. "Probably," she said. "But all the same, while I'm out here, I'd like to see something."

"You shall," he promised, his voice grim. "I'll organize a safari just for you."

"But wouldn't it cost an awful lot?" she asked him quickly.

He smiled at that. "No — we'll have a 'busman's holiday' one of these days. Just the four of us. You, Fenella, me and Dan. Isn't that a good idea?"

She looked at him and wondered if it was. The less she saw of him the better for her — and yet at the same time, she could not bear not to see him.

"It's a wonderful idea," she said, and he wondered why she sounded depressed.

8

IT was incredible how fast the days flew by. The nights were still bad but during the frightening night hours Hilary learned to read by the flickering light of the lamp and to sleep heavily in the hot hours at midday.

Since her cocktail-party, she had felt herself surrounded by friends. Every day someone either called to see her — or fetched her in their car for lunch, or telephoned her. She knew that at any hour she could go to the telephone and would soon be hearing Anna's friendly voice or listen to Mrs. Adams's platitudes delivered in that majestic manner, or even — if she wanted to, could talk to Philip himself. Wanted to? She longed to, with a deep hungry ache that shocked her and that made her more determined than ever to leave Africa.

One of the first things she did was to start a long letter to her mother. It was not an easy letter to write. To be truthful yet tactful, was not easy. Somehow she must make her mother see the situation through Fay's eyes so that she could understand; yet fairness to Dan demanded that she not exaggerate the situation. Hilary, herself, could not see why Fay was so unhappy, so desperately in need of money, but then Hilary recognized that she and her sister were two totally different characters. Where Hilary could be happy, Fay would be miserable; what Hilary saw as riches, would make Fay discontented. The letter was started and crumpled up a dozen times. But finally Hilary wrote one that she felt might meet the situation. Her mother was good at reading between the lines and perhaps she would understand better than her daughters expected.

Before the letter could be posted, however, Dan and Fay returned.

Hilary had been sitting on the thatched *stoep*, watching the tiny brightly-coloured birds as they flitted from flower to flower — with their crimson and aquamarine bodies and long honey beaks — and enjoying their gay chatter when she heard the sound of a Rover. She fled indoors, hastily combing her hair and 'doing' her face. Her heart thumping uncomfortably, she sauntered back to the *stoep*, hoping, against hope — and yet dreading — that it might be Philip.

She was ridiculously disappointed to see Dan clamber out of the Rover.

"Hey," he called out. "Still alive?"

Fay came round the back of the Rover. She looked dusty and irritable.

"You look very pleased with life," she greeted Hilary. "Who did you think it was?"

"Philip," Hilary said truthfully.

Fay snorted a little, pulling off her hat, rubbing her eyes. "Am I tired. Dan drove like a madman, just because he's annoyed with me."

"Annoyed!" Dan shouted over his shoulder. He was opening the drink cabinet and pouring himself out a drink, shouting for Petrus to bring iced water, warding off the affectionate caresses of a wildly excited Samson. "I'm bloody mad," he said furiously. "Effie had to play the fool and get the wife all worked up with jealousy."

"Simply because I was polite to the poor man," Fay said with acid sweetness,

150

"was there any need for her to behave like a child afraid of losing her toy? In any case, she deserves to lose him. If ever there was a dumb nitwit — and just look at her. Ankles like tree trunks and figure like a beer barrel."

"All the same, he is her husband," Dan pointed out.

Hilary sat, clenching her hands, her body taut. If only they would stop shouting at one another. The pleasant restfulness of the place had vanished in a moment and now the air was crackling with hostility. The way they glared at one another; the cruel cutting things they both said — how could they ever pick up the pieces after such a quarrel and behave as if nothing had happened? Yet they could.

Today was no exception. Fay had first bath and she came to sit on the *stoep* with Hilary while Dan showered.

"Have you been very bored and lonely?" Fay asked languidly She wore a green silk négligé and green feathered mules. She had washed her hair and pinned up the long damp coil into a comical knot on top of her head. She wore no make-up and yet she looked unbelievably lovely, Hilary thought.

"No, I've met quite a few local people," Hilary began, happy to see that Fay was in a better mood. And then she remembered. "Oh, Fay, I almost forgot. A man called to see you. His name was . . . " She had to hunt in her memory for a moment, "Carlos Antunes . . . "

Fay dropped the bottle of nail-varnish with which she had been painting her nails. Every drop of blood drained out of her face. "What did he want?" Her voice was husky.

"He wouldn't say. He said he'd write or telephone you. He . . . "

Fay was looking over her shoulder. Now she grabbed Hilary's arm . . . "tell me later," she said huskily just as Dan came out.

He had shaved and was in clean clothes and looked much happier. He sat down and stretched out his legs. "What were you girls chattering about? 'Pon my word, you sound like birds twittering. What's so exciting?"

Fay smiled. "Hilary was telling me she's been meeting some of the neighbours."

"Is that a fact?" Dan grinned at her. "Good for you. How did it happen?"

"Philip took me to a cocktail-party," Hilary said, wondering why she felt so reluctant to mention Philip's name. "I met a lot of people there and since then, they are always telephoning me or coming to see me. I like Anna very much . . . "

"I won't have her in this house," Fay said with startling abruptness. "This is my house, Hilary, you've no right to ask your friends here."

"But . . . " Hilary began in dismay.

Dan was grinning. "Did you meet the handsome husband? What did you think of him?"

"Rather conceited," Hilary said honestly and was taken aback by Dan's shout of delighted laughter. She turned to Fay and was shocked at the look on her sister's face.

"Shut up you . . . you baboon . . . " Fay said, getting up and kicking over her chair as she went into the house.

Dan finished out his laughter and then looked at Hilary's tight little unhappy face. "Sorry, Hilary," he said gravely. "I

153

didn't mean to make her mad. Don't you know why Fay hates Anna so? Can't you guess?"

She shook her head. He narrowed his eyes and gave her a pitying smile.

"Forget it. You're so damned young . . . " He stood up. "I'm going in to get the post if my lady wife deigns to wonder where I am." He had gone before she remembered her still unposted letter to her mother. Oh well, it could go another day.

As if she had been waiting for a signal, Fay came out of the house as soon as the dusty Rover had gone. She still looked pale and anxious. "Now tell me about Carlos. When did he come — were you alone?"

"It was about eleven one morning. I was quite alone and was gardening with Simon —"

Hilary described how Petrus had come running to find her, how she had hastily washed her hands and gone out to the *stoep*, there to see the most amazing car: a Cadillac, all pale blue and gleaming despite the dust, and a tall, dark man waiting. But she did not describe the queer effect the man had had on her with his slightly foreign accent, his swarthy skin and those queer eyes. She did not say that the way he had stared at her had frightened her, that she found herself staring back at him, unable to drag her eyes away. She told her sister how he had spoken almost arrogantly, as if annoyed to find that Fay was away; had demanded to know when she would return.

"I had a strong impression that he had expected you to be here, Fay," Hilary finished, "and was annoyed about it."

"But I told him . . . " Fay began and stopped. She gave a light, very artificial laugh. "Forget it, Hilary. I met him at a party and he asked if he could call on me one day. You know what foreigners are — so gallant and attentive. I found him very attractive, didn't you?"

Hilary shivered. "Not very."

Fay laughed, a more genuine laugh this time. "You don't like your men too sophisticated, is that it? Look, don't mention it to Dan — he's so infernally jealous."

Hilary looked at her anxiously. "Dan is so nice, Fay . . . "

"You think so?" Fay laughed. "You should try being married to him and you'd change your mind. Moody! . . . "

"So are you."

Fay half-frowned. "But . . . " The telephone bell shrilled. Fay laughed. "How the grape vine works. I bet you that's one of my so-called friends welcoming me home."

Fay was away a considerable time but Hilary was quite happy to sit there alone, scratching Samson's head, staring at the distant plain below them. There was a wonderful clarity in the air and she could see small groups of thorn trees and minute *koppies*. The sky was not blue — it was too pale to be called blue — but it had a dazzling quality about it.

Fay had tried to make light of it but undoubtedly she, too, was afraid of the mysterious Carlos Antunes. Who could he be and in what connexion had he called on Fay? He was obviously used to people being where he expected to find them — and also obviously annoyed to find she wasn't. The story about meeting at a cocktail-party was too weak for

156

words. Fay must have been badly rattled not to have thought of a better story. Hilary shivered despite the heat. She hoped Carlos Antunes would keep away — away from both her and from Fay. A man with such cruel, evil, frightening eyes was one best avoided.

Fay came back, her face patchy with anger. "So you've been having a good time with Philip," she began. "Why didn't you tell me?"

Hilary stared at her, startled and dismayed. "But Fay, you're only just home. I told you Philip took me to a cocktail-party and . . . "

"But not that you lunched alone at his house."

"That was after church. It was only because the service was late and . . . "

"Everyone's talking about it." Fay flushed again. "They didn't waste much time letting me know."

Hilary was rarely moved to anger but suddenly she was. "Look, Fay," she said quickly, "I'm twenty and not a child. What do they want to ring you up about it for? Philip is a decent man and I'm not a fool — what harm was there in lunching with him?"

Fay stared at her for a long silent moment and then shrugged. "How right you are," she drawled slowly, "what harm could there be in it! He was sorry for you, of course."

"Not only sorry, but mad because I was left alone," Hilary went on, her cheeks flushed now with anger.

"I suppose he blamed Dan — "

Hilary took a deep breath. "I wouldn't let him. Why should Dan take the blame that was . . . " She stopped herself in time. She was shaking all over and felt sick and horrified with herself. She had nearly said the unforgivable thing — had nearly told Fay the truth: that she was completely and utterly selfish.

"I hope you told him it was your own idea," Fay went on. "If not, I certainly shall."

Hilary felt her shoulders sag. She was suddenly very weary.

"Fay — " she changed the subject abruptly. "I want to go back to England. I'm not happy here and you don't need me."

Fay stared at her. "But Hilary . . . "

158

Hilary shook her head. "It's no good, Fay. My mind is made up. I came out, thinking to help you but you don't need me and I'm only a drag on the budget." She stood and Samson moved to her side, leaning against her. His warmth was vaguely comforting. "It's better if I go home."

Fay was looking at her with real dismay. "Oh, no . . . " she began and then they both heard the Rover.

"Dan hasn't been long," Hilary said, wishing she could slip away to her room, feeling her flesh start to tingle with fear of the scenes that would inevitably start.

Dan came with the leather bag which he tipped up on to the table, beginning to sort the letters. "There's a cable here for you, Hilary. It must have gone to the wrong address, they say, for it's taken a hell of a time to get here apparently."

Hilary wondered why her mother was cabling her. It could be from no one else.

She stared at the words, unable to believe them, reading and re-reading them over and over again.

Your mother died yesterday. Don't come home. Am writing. Father.

She felt suddenly very cold — and then very hot. She heard Dan's voice from a long way away as she put out a blind hand. It could not be true. Mother . . . It could not be — it must not be . . .

When she came round, she was lying on the bed, with Dan hovering anxiously over her and Fay looking almost disdainfully amused at the fuss he was making.

Hilary opened her eyes. "Did I faint?" she said wonderingly. "I've never fainted before."

"There always has to be a first time for everything," Fay pointed out sweetly.

Dan glared at her. "Shut up or get out," he said savagely. He turned to Hilary. "It was a terrible shock for you," he said. "Was your mother so ill?"

Hilary pushed back her hair. "She suffered from anaemia and was not strong. She got very tired so she had to take things easily but I thought . . . I mean, we none of us guessed . . . "

Fay had vanished. Now she called.

160

"There's two letters here for you, Hilary. One is from Father."

It was an effort to walk out to the *stoep*, to take the letter and open it with shaking hands. Then she looked at the others. "If — if you don't mind, I'd like to read this alone."

"Don't forget," Fay said quickly, "that he's my father as well."

It was a very long letter, written in his neat, slightly backward sloping writing. It was not an affectionate letter but then Hilary would not have expected affection from her father. He had never shown any, so why start now?

It was a letter written by a man who was deeply shocked, bewildered and angry, as well as grieved.

I cannot understand how your mother could do such a thing to me, taking her own life when she knows how I feel about suicides.

Suicide. The ugly word made Hilary shudder. Why — what could have happened to have made her mother take her own life? It made it all a million times worse.

She read on:

When I found her, sleeping, as I thought, so peacefully, I was merely pleased that she had overcome her chronic insomnia from which, as doubtless you know, she has suffered all our married life. Then, when I could not awaken her — I had an urgent message from the Bishop and had to wake your mother to pack my suitcase for me — I grew alarmed. I shook her and then realized that something was wrong. I sent for the doctor. He is a new man. Hard, impatient, he asked why I had not tried respiration. I said that I had no idea that she was dead. I had thought her asleep. He tried for an hour then took your mother to hospital but it was too late.

As you can imagine I am lost without her. I find the attitude of my parishioners extremely strange. There is no sympathy or human kindness in the village. My only friend is Maggie Soar. She is now my right hand. I have sent you a cable not to come home as I am going to America.

The Bishop, who realizes how I feel, has given me an important mission. I am to preach throughout the United States and he wishes me to leave immediately after the funeral. Maggie is storing our furniture and very kindly sorting out your mother's personal belongings. There is a new Vicar coming here. The Bishop feels my vocation lies in preaching rather than in parochial work.

I shall continue paying your sister twenty pounds a month towards your keep . . .

Hilary lowered the letter and took a deep breath. Why had Fay lied to her? Let her think she was a drag on the housekeeping? Twenty pounds would more than pay for her keep. Was that why Fay had seemed so dismayed to learn she planned to leave? Ashamed of the unkind thought, Hilary read on:

I feel this is an excessive sum but your mother insisted that the cost of living was extremely high in Africa and as it was her wish . . . I have always understood from your mother that if she should die, both you and your sister would be well provided for so I do not feel any compunction at all about not sending you money. No doubt if you are ever in need, I shall hear from you.

I shall not send any message to your sister for I no longer feel she is my child. She is, unfortunately, a throwback to a less pleasing side of our family. Your mother's brother, whom you, fortunately, never met, and your sister are very similar. Both completely amoral. Not immoral, I said amoral. If you do not know the difference, it is time you did so and I would suggest you purchase a dictionary. Both, as I have said, completely amoral and ruthless, egoistical, seeing no other person's right save their own. Your mother's brother died on the gallows. He murdered an old lady after squandering her savings. It would not surprise me in the least if your sister did the same. I saw it when she was a child; I tried to restrain her selfish inclinations, to teach her what was right and wrong. I failed completely. I am telling you this, my daughter, because I wish to warn you. Even though you are her sister, if you threaten what she believes to be her 'happiness', she will have no mercy.

I would like you to leave her when the Will is proved and you are independent and try to make a new life for yourself in Rhodesia or South Africa. As soon as I have one I will send you a permanent address which will always find me.

Hilary folded the letter carefully and replaced it in the envelope. She lay, staring at the ceiling. How strange that her father should warn her against Fay. How he misjudged poor Fay. Just because she had been gay and loving, wanting freedom and the normal life the average girl is allowed to enjoy, he had decided she was . . . what was his word? Amoral.

She opened the second letter. It was from Maggie Soar.

My poor child, she read. I know what a terrible shock this is to you, but not, believe me, a greater one than it was to us all. Your father, who found it so difficult to show affection while she lived, is like a bird with one wing. It is terrible to see how it has affected him. I am glad the dear Bishop is sending him to new lands, and the difficult assignment I understand he has been given will surely be the best cure for his heartbreak.

Now I must tell you that your mother did a very brave, unselfish thing when she took what is commonly called the 'coward's' way out. We believed, always, that she suffered from anaemia. We have just learned that it was her heart and that she had suffered severe pain. It had grown rapidly worse and she knew that she had not long to live and that her last months might see her, not only a complete invalid, but suffering recurrent heart attacks. She told me once that, as a young girl, she had nursed an elderly aunt through a long painful illness and that it had left a scar on her she could never lose. She said that she prayed for a quick death so that you would not be shackled to her side and forced to see her die in agony. That is why I think she sent you to Africa for she knew her days were numbered. She took sleeping pills so you need not think she died in pain.

Your father seems to think God will not admit her to Heaven because she took her life which is a sin. My God is a different God — I think He will understand and to understand is to forgive. Your mother was the noblest, most unselfish, kind woman I have ever known. God will remember that. I hope you are happy. I doubt anyone could be happy with Fay. She is too like your father in his egoism and ruthless determination to have his own way. I am sorry for him now but sometimes I remember the way your mother slaved in that great Rectory — this is when you were younger and she was not ill.

I understand from your mother that she was making your father financially secure for she could not bear him to be worried about money, but that the bulk of her inheritance has been left to you girls. I am not sure how the Will is worded but I imagine you will get two-thirds as Fay has a husband, and if either of you die, the other sister will get the money. But you will not wish to think of money now.

Hilary, my child, your mother left a

note in which she wrote: 'Tell Hilary not to grieve. This is the best way. I shall always be near her.' Now, my dear, good-bye. I am sorting out your mother's personal things and will pack them to send to you as soon as you ask for them. She was a dear soul and we are all missing her very much indeed.

Hilary finished reading. Slowly she folded the letter. Fay stood in the doorway, her eyes bright.

"What does Father say?" Her hand was out-stretched for the letter.

Hilary hesitated, trying to remember all her father had said. Fay would not like the bit about Uncle Charles. "It's my letter," she said stubbornly. "I don't want you to read it."

Fay's face flamed. "I'm going to read it. I suppose you've been left all the money . . . " Her voice was bitter.

Hilary felt the tears suddenly very near. She jumped up, flung her father's letter at Fay and walked out of the room, through the house and out of it, just as Philip walked in, his face grave.

"I've just heard, Hilary." He saw her

blind stricken look and he caught her by the arm. "Come with me," he said gently and helped her in the Rover, turning it quickly and driving away.

He drove silently while Hilary kept her head turned and stared blindly out of the window. She would not cry . . . she would not . . . would not. She bit her lip and blinked her eyes fiercely. She would not cry.

Gradually the inward surging subsided and she could blow her nose and even manage a faint smile. "Where are we going?"

"I'm going to show you something," he told her.

She remembered then that she had left Maggie Soar's letter behind as well. Not that it would matter if Fay did read it. There was nothing in the letter to hurt her.

Philip parked the Rover in the sparse shade of a thorn tree. He helped Hilary out, looked approvingly at her shoes and announced that they were going to take a walk. He had a gun under his arm and with the other hand he took her elbow. They walked over the hot sandy veldt slowly, bypassing thorn trees, Philip's eyes intent on the ground. It was very hot and she felt the perspiration beginning to run down her back. Yet the rhythmic movement of their walking was a comforting release for her taut nerves. She walked, thinking of nothing but putting the next foot forward and then the next. She did not know how long she walked in silence until suddenly, he halted her.

They were standing in a clump of thorn trees. "Look," Philip said very softly.

She shook her head, trying to focus her eyes. All they had seen before was the sandy ground. As she stared in the direction in which he pointed, she saw a herd of zebra. They were standing round a small pool. How extraordinarily neat their stripes were, she thought absurdly, just as if they had been painted on with the aid of a ruler. Philip turned her round gently and pointed in another direction. This time it was harder — but at last she saw several wildebeeste with their great shoulders. They were moving slowly but as if with a definite goal in view. A couple of small snowy birds with long white necks flew round and alighted on the broad backs of the wildebeeste.

"Egrets," Philip said in her ear, "but they are commonly called tick-birds for obvious reasons."

He took a big white hankie out of his pocket and spread it on the ground for her to sit on; then drew out a thermos of iced water from the pack over his shoulder and gave her a long drink.

"Listen," he said.

She listened. At first there was nothing to hear. Just silence. And then she began to distinguish different noises. The quiet munching of an animal eating; the grass, sparse and rough, rustling slightly in the almost imperceptible breeze; the sudden chirruping of a cicada. The zebra were still drinking placidly, some moving farther away. The wildebeeste were nearly out of sight, growing smaller and smaller. A huge vulture suddenly flapped out of a nearby tree, its hideous bald neck and ugly head flopping as he flew through the trees.

Philip stood up and helped her to her feet. "We'd better get going. You don't usually walk into lions at this spot but it looks as if somewhere there has been a kill. I don't want you to see your first lion at such close quarters." He grinned at her.

She looked at him with the trusting eyes of a child "I'm not afraid," she said simply. He realized that she had received such a shock that all her ordinary inhibitions had vanished.

"Why not?" he asked gently.

She smiled at him. "Because I'm with you."

Her head was tilted back, her face had the same inviting, child-like look that had caused him to kiss her after the dance. He had a strange illogical desire to take her in his arms, to comfort that sad little face, to hold that thin body close, to cherish her.

The word shook him back to sanity. "We'd better get moving," he said almost harshly. "They'll be wondering where you are."

Still in a dream, she obeyed and began to walk. They walked, as before, in silence. But their thoughts were completely different.

She was aware of a great sense of peace. The shock and sorrow at her mother's death had miraculously vanished; the lies that Fay had told did not matter for now their mother knew and would forgive them. She had a feeling that her mother was at peace, was happy. The exercise, the quiet vastness of the veldt, the sight of the wild animals moving so completely unaware of onlookers, had given her a serenity she had not known for a long time.

Philip's thoughts were very different. Fenella had telephoned to tell him of their mother's death. "I can't understand Hilary," she had said, "she doesn't seem to care." He had known, instinctively, that such a remark could not be true. Fenella might not believe it. She was so amazingly lacking in imagination that she rarely understood how other people felt. Remembering how Hilary had talked of her mother, he had known how shocked and grieved she would be; how hard she would try to hide it. So he had rushed over.

That was the first strange thing he had done. The second had been that

moment when he had wanted to take
her in his arms and — and 'cherish'
her. What an odd word for him to
have used. Surely he was not falling
in love with Hilary? Glancing down at
her small figure, walking so valiantly,
he was amazed at himself. He liked his
women witty and sophisticated, a little
hard, maybe, ruthless, but vitally alive.
Like Fenella. Unconsciously he hastened
his steps so that Hilary had to almost run.
Yes, Fenella was the kind of woman he
could love.

9

ONCE again the days slid by, almost imperceptibly becoming weeks; but this time not because Hilary felt ill or led a secluded life, merely because there always seemed so much to do.

After Philip had taken her home that day she was always to remember — when she learned her mother was dead and, later, in the quietness of the bush veldt, she had found serenity, Fay had hardly mentioned their mother. Once she had burst out angrily during a meal: "I don't see why you get two-thirds of the money."

And Dan said in an icy voice: "Because you're married and your husband is supposed to keep you."

Fay gave her taunting laugh. "That's good, I must say. 'Supposed' is certainly the operative word."

Hilary, her cheeks burning, her eyes worried, tried to make peace but the two ignored her. Fay went on taunting Dan.

"I little thought I'd be reduced to this sort of life — "

"You chose it."

"With my eyes blindfolded."

"I never lied to you — "

"You never told me the truth!"

And quite suddenly Dan stood up, sending the chair crashing to the floor. "For God's sake, shut up," he shouted. "If you don't like this life, get out. You'll have independent means, now." He slammed out of the room and they heard the roar of the Land Rover as it whizzed down the hill.

Fay laughed quite happily and began eating grapes.

Hilary looked at her. "I believe you enjoy these rows," she said wonderingly.

Fay looked across the table, her eyes dancing. "Of course I do. It keeps us alive."

After that, Hilary managed to develop a self-protective attitude towards the rows. They could rage all round her and she would sit, a smile nailed to her face, reminding herself that they enjoyed fighting.

Now that she knew so many people in the neighbourhood, Hilary found herself constantly being asked out. She learned to drive the old car but often people came to fetch her. Occasionally Fay went as well to the teas or the cocktail-parties, but often sent Hilary alone.

"These people bore me," she would say, yawning. "Time I saw some new faces."

So Hilary went alone and thoroughly enjoyed herself. She became quite fond of Mrs. Adams, despite her 'Duchess' manner and of course, her friendship with Anna increased. This was a real bone of contention with Fay.

"I won't have that woman in my house," she would say violently.

"But why not?"

Fay's face went blank, she stared blindly out of the window, and then looked at Hilary imploringly, her voice suddenly young. "It's her face, Hilary. I can't bear to look at that dreadful birthmark."

"But I hardly notice it. You get used to it."

Fay shuddered. "I can never get

used to ugliness."

Hilary suppressed a sigh of impatience. All people were not blessed with Fay's warm beauty; surely it would not hurt her to be civil to Anna? But no, Fay would not go to a party if she knew Anna would be there. In the end Hilary would go alone to Anna's small timber house and spend a quiet afternoon with her, both content to knit and chat, or just to sit in the shade and gaze at the wonderful view.

There was always so much for Hilary to see. She had agreed to postpone her departure until the Will was proved, for she knew that Fay would sorely miss the twenty pounds a month; yet all the same, she felt she was in Africa on borrowed time, and as the weeks passed her impatience to leave the stickily hot country increased. She was not unhappy; people were too friendly for that. Nor was she bored; there were a million things to see. Now that Philip had introduced her to the game, a new world was open. Her eyes grew accustomed to focusing and she would spend hours on the little veranda searching the distant plain, the binoculars to her eyes, her excitement mounting when she caught sight of a graceful buck leaping, or a group of giraffes, their long bodies oddly hunching as they galloped with their weird, slow-motion movements. Once Dan drove her to a water hole and they hid in a clump of thick trees, sitting tense and silent, waiting. A group of giraffes had come to drink and it had been all she could do not to laugh as she watched the awkward way they spreadeagled their front legs and slowly sank to the ground to drink. Even as they watched, some buck also came to drink — thin, frail-looking creatures with enormous dark eyes, their heads turning with clean, quick, frightened movements.

A very good friendship had grown up between Hilary and Dan. He knew how much she enjoyed seeing the game and he went out of his way to take her out. Fay, of course, declared she had seen too much game, she did not care if she never saw another lion.

There were many things about Dan that Hilary liked. His protective manner and his air of treating her as though she were very young and precious. What worried her, was the loneliness she saw in his eyes. She felt absurdly responsible. Just because Fay was her sister, it was not her fault if Fay could not make Dan happy; yet she still wanted to say the right thing to Dan; to have his eyes light up with pleasure if she praised something he did; to encourage his eagerness to talk about this land that seemed to him to be paradise on earth. Hilary loved to get him to talk about the Africans. He spoke as a father might; chiding them for their faults but with great tolerance.

"They can be a lazy lot of devils," he would say, "but maybe they're right. Why do we spend all our lives rushing round madly, trying to save a couple of minutes? Maybe they do lie and steal — maybe they are unreliable, but we have to remember the very thin veneer of education they have had. They're sub-normal, really; mere children. Some of my scouts are fine fellows yet they're absolutely slaves to the witch doctors."

He told her about these creatures. "They throw the bones and foretell what will happen. Oddly enough, it often does." He shook his head thoughtfully. "If a tree or cow is struck by lightning, no African will move it until it has been cleansed by a witch doctor. If your crops die, if you fall ill — it means someone has *magicked* you and so you send for the witch doctor to make a bigger spell for you."

"And they really believe it?"

Dan grinned. "Of course. Why not? Don't tell me you haven't seen people walk out into a busy road in London to avoid going under a ladder? Or throw spilt salt over their shoulders? Or cross their fingers? Well, if we do things like that after generations of education, why blame the African?"

"Fay speaks their language very well."

A cloud passed over Dan's face. "Damned well. Sometimes I wonder . . ." He hesitated. "Doesn't she run a sort of clinic?"

"Oh yes, every day she has several patients. Knife wounds, broken heads, and so on. She's extraordinarily clever with them. Funny, I'd never have expected it of Fay. Not the Fay I used to know."

They were walking down a narrow track and Dan paused to hold back a long thorny branch so that Hilary could pass by. "She's changed," he said grimly. "She's had to — ".

★ ★ ★

Hilary loved to sit on the veranda in the morning, watching the stream of Africans climb the hill, pass the house and go on down the track that led to a small Indian-owned store. They were so colourful, some of them. Tall Africans with bright squares tucked over one shoulder, with skin skirts carrying great oval shields and knobkerries as they walked, heads high, features arrogant, followed — at a distance by their numerous wives, each carrying a load on her head, often having a baby strapped to her back in a thick blanket. Sometimes the women wore European clothes; very bright frocks with gay head scarves, the babies in pink sunbonnets, their heads nodding as their mothers walked.

Hilary loved to waken early and go outside and watch the pearly sky change colour until suddenly the sun rose, a huge golden dazzling ball, to mount rapidly in the blue sky. She loved to sit very still, Samson by her side, as he grunted in his sleep, his tongue a small pink curly tip showing in his half-open mouth, as she watched some weird insect — a praying mantis perhaps, or a fascinating stick insect; or even a great green locust, his sharp teeth chewing a leaf, his long serrated legs folded on his back.

Sometimes she would stroll round the back of the house to the rondavel where Fay held the clinic. Fay would wear her white coat, her blonde head hidden by a white scarf, her face almost dedicated. She worked fast — listening to the African's complaint, waiting patiently, yet with her eyes wandering over the waiting crowd, asking Carl to interpret if she could not understand. Then she would look at the wound or the ulcer, or where the pain was said to be — and in a moment, she would either bathe the wound, put ointment on or produce medicine and the African would be passed on to Carl, who would take the sixpence.

"Never do anything for an African for nothing," Fay told Hilary. "They think it's no good if it's free. They appreciate what they have to pay for."

"You should have been a nurse," Hilary said one day, lost in admiration of the way Fay had stopped the bleeding of a deep knife wound and had bandaged it.

Fay shuddered. "I'd loathe it."

"Yet you like this — " Hilary waved her hand vaguely.

Fay looked at her with a half-smile. "Like it? I think that's putting it rather strongly. They're useful to me and I'm useful to them, that's all it amounts to." She looked startled as if surprised at what she had said. "Someone has to do it," she finished rather lamely.

Her words puzzled Hilary for a long time. What use were those sick Africans to Fay? Or did she mean that they kept her busy — kept her from being bored?

There were many things that puzzled Hilary.

Philip's behaviour, for one thing. After he had taken her home from seeing her first wild game, he stayed for a drink, but from that day on, he had never

184

been near the house. Several times Dan had remarked, half-jokingly, that Hilary seemed to have driven Philip away, but Fay had said quickly and irritably, that Philip had something better to do than pay social calls. Yet wherever Hilary went to cocktail parties, dinners — there she saw Philip. And, stranger still, he seemed to make a bee line for her. It embarrassed her a little, for Mrs. Adams teased her several times about it — and even Anna had said thoughtfully that it was a pity Hilary disliked Philip so much, for he ought to marry.

Hilary flushed. "I don't dislike him. It's just . . . just that he's so moody. You never know where you are with him. One day friendly, the next biting your head off."

Anna laughed. "As bad as that?" She no longer tried to keep the unblemished side of her face towards Hilary; she sensed that Hilary no longer noticed the birthmark.

It seemed odd, sometimes, to Hilary, driving down the twisting lane, Samson by her side, to think that she was in 'darkest Africa'. A land of jungles and lion-haunted plains, with elephant country not far away, with snakes lying in wait on the branches of the trees, with scorpions, fighter ants, a thousand dangerous creatures nearby — yet here she was, going to a cocktail-party that might be taking place in any town in the world. She knew that if the party ended late, one of the men would drive home behind her to see that she was all right. She knew that they would all stand about the room, the men in little groups talking 'shop', the women grumbling about their servants or comparing their children.

Hilary had already met the 'Jackie' of the photographs Fay had sent home of her 'own' child. That was another odd thing about Fay. She had said abruptly one day soon after they learned of their mother's death: "Now Mother need never know the truth." She had sounded quite cheerful. "I was so afraid," Fay had gone on, "that your stupid, priggish conscience would make you tell her, and it might have been awkward."

Fay did not mind in the least having lied. That was the truth of it. Nor did she feel relieved because their mother had not had to be hurt by learning the truth. She was relieved because there would be no 'awkwardness'. Surely Fay realized that now their mother was dead, she must know the truth?

Fay's outlook on life constantly puzzled Hilary. They saw almost everything through different eyes.

One morning, Hilary strolled round to the 'clinic' and saw Fay talking earnestly to an old crone of an African woman. She was stooped like a fairy tale witch, her hand clutching a long stick, her face wrinkled, with its beady eyes peering up at Fay's face, her mud-streaked hair half-hidden by a dirty cloth, her thin body covered by a dun-coloured blanket. Fay was talking earnestly and the old woman was nodding her head. She held up her other hand showing five fingers, closing it and repeating the gesture several times. Fay laughed and shook her head vigorously. She held up five fingers twice and said something. The old crone in her turn shook her head. Her voice sounded clearly.

"Aieee . . . Aiee . . . " she cried sadly.

Fay laughed and then saw Hilary. She

frowned. "What do you want?" she asked sharply.

Hilary felt uncomfortable. Did Fay think she was 'snooping'?

"I was just wandering around. What does she want?"

Fay was still frowning as she turned away. "Only to sell me something and she expects me to pay a fantastic sum. Well, I'm not going to . . ."

The old woman walked away with shuffling steps, grasping her stick, her voice still sounding clear as she kept saying: "Aiee . . . Aiee . . ."

Seeing that she was not wanted, for already Fay was in the rondavel, looking at her array of bottles, Hilary wandered back to the front of the house. That was another thing about Fay that vaguely worried her — her secretiveness. What could Fay have that was so precious? She was always locking up a room or a drawer or a cupboard. She carried the keys attached to her belt. She was always writing letters and hastily covering them if Hilary entered the room — she was often on the telephone, abruptly ending the conversation if Hilary appeared.

All small things but they added up to an uncomfortable total. Hilary felt that she was either unwanted — or else Fay was doing something she did not want Hilary to know about. Either solution was guaranteed to make her feel intensely uncomfortable and eager to be out of the house. She began to long for the Will to be proved and everything settled. She often wished she had never left England — but the next moment, knew that this was not true. She would not have missed the experience of seeing Africa or the chance of meeting Philip.

There was a dance held at Monsimbe one Saturday night. Dan, Fay and Hilary went to it. It was very gay with coloured lanterns and streamers to throw, plenty to drink and a crowded floor. Hilary enjoyed every moment of it. She had no lack of partners; being the only young unmarried girl in the room all the young men vied for her. She danced with Philip, her pulse racing, her mouth dry as she heard herself prattling away to him and wishing she could stop. He had such a strange effect on her, she thought worriedly. She always wanted to please him and never succeeded; doing, in fact, all the things most likely to irritate him.

"When are you going back to England?" he asked curtly as they samba-ed.

She was busy trying to follow him. "I don't know."

"Fenella told me you wanted to go."

"Oh, I do," Hilary said earnestly, shaking back the dark curls that were clinging damply to her head. Although it was late at night, it was intensely hot, the only air coming from the whirring fans overhead.

"Why? Are you unhappy here?"

She considered the question. "Not . . . not really, but . . . but I don't feel I fit in here, somehow."

The music stopped and they were at one end of the room. He got her a drink and led the way to the chairs. She felt very conspicuous and wondered how she could join the rest of the party without it being too obvious.

"Why?" he asked.

Hilary looked at him thoughtfully. "I . . . I haven't any proper job to do here," she said rather lamely. "I thought . . . " She stopped just in time. She had been going to say that she had thought she could help Fay but of course, that was getting dangerously near the subject of the lies she was supposed to have told about Fay's child. "Fay doesn't need me and . . . and . . . I'm sure they'd be happier without me."

Philip's eyes were narrowed. "You're not the cause of their quarrels."

She could feel the colour in her cheeks. So he knew! As if he could read her thoughts, he gave a grunting sort of laugh. "They've always quarrelled, you know, it means very little."

"Oh, that's what I think," she said, with that breathless little rush he remembered so well. "It worried me terribly at first but . . . but I'm beginning to think they enjoy it."

He grinned. "A queer kind of enjoyment."

She smiled. "That's what I feel. I — I couldn't bear it."

He flexed his hands, staring down at his fingers. "You're happy?"

This was the Philip she liked. The sympathetic, serious, friendly Philip. She was tempted to tell him the truth — yet hesitated. His mood could easily change.

"I am — and I'm not . . . " She looked at him with her huge dark eyes. "I — I feel kind of . . . spare. If you know what I mean."

He looked at her. She was still far too thin and a small pulse was jumping in her temple as if she was nervous. Was she still fretting for that man who had jilted her? Fenella had said only that evening how difficult Hilary was these days; irritable, bored, hard to please, easily upset. Fenella had also said a strange thing that he had found hard to believe and yet Fenella must know her own sister. She had said that Hilary was 'man-mad' — that she was even trying to have an *affaire* with Dan. He had been shocked and a little angry.

"She's too young and I'm sure she wouldn't look at a married man."

Fenella had laughed — almost sadly. "My poor Philip, how easily a man is fooled," she had said. "That little lost waif stunt of Hilary's gets them every time. She's got Dan running in circles round her and now it looks as if you . . . " She had shaken her head at him. "Poor little Hilary. It must have been such a shock — such a public humiliation. No wonder she has to have every man eating out of her hand just to boost her morale."

"But Dan . . . "

"She looks at him adoringly, hangs on to his every word, gets him to take her out to see wild animals, is horribly scared. Oh, you know the usual line. Only it upsets me, Philip. She used to be such a sweet, unaffected kid — I hate that man for what he did to her," she had finished almost fiercely.

Looking down at the rather sad little face, Philip echoed the sentiments. But Hilary was young and healthy; it was morbid to cling to the past. How could he make her see that without letting her know he knew about her cancelled wedding?

"Look," he said now almost harshly. "The past is finished — forget it. Your whole life is before you. You want to look forward and not back."

She stared at him, startled by his vehemence. "Oh, I don't know," she said quickly and saw that he did not believe her. "I — I mean . . . I loved Mother dearly but . . . but she had been ill for so long and . . . "

His eyes narrowed again. There she was, twisting things deliberately. He had not meant her mother's death. She had got over that with surprising ease — another thing that Fenella could not understand.

"There's a tough streak about Hilary that you wouldn't suspect," she had told Philip on one of their meetings in Monsimbe. "I think I miss Mother far more."

The music started and unconsciously Hilary's foot began to tap. Philip glanced down the room at the group of young men near the bar, several gazing their way. "I mustn't monopolize you," he said. "You'd prefer to dance with some of those attentive young men."

Without thought she answered, "I'd prefer to dance with you."

He stood up and held out his hands, smiling a little ruefully. So Fenella was right. Any man was worth trying for — what a very naïve remark. Did she really think a man would fall for it? Yet coupled with that rapt look she wore as she danced, her eyes half-closed, any man would be forgiven for swallowing it. He was glad when the music came to an end and they were near the bar and he could murmur an excuse and leave her, knowing a dozen men were waiting to take his place.

He went out on to the long veranda to cool off. There was a round orange moon in the sky and a billion stars seemed to be winking. He wiped his damp forehead and hands, thinking how he had been fooled. He had seen Hilary as a rather sweet child but now, he was beginning to wonder.

A hand on his arm made him turn. It was Fenella herself. She came to stand close beside him, her hand by her side, feeling for his fingers, her full skirt hiding their clasped hands from curious eyes.

"Philip — I must see you alone . . . " she said with desperate quietness that startled him.

"Fenella, I thought we agreed . . . You shouldn't be out here now . . . " he said in dismay. Their small community was so quick to gossip, and scandal here flew throughout the district like a flame and was hard to combat or live down.

"I had to speak to you." Her voice trembled. "I thought you loved me. You've hardly been near me. Dancing all the time with Hilary . . ."

"Three times," he said drily.

"I know I've no right to be jealous," Fenella went on, "but I still am. That's the heartbreaking part of it. Oh, Philip — why did we ever have to meet?"

His hand tightened on hers. "I'm not sorry, darling."

She half-turned. He was horribly aware of the eyes that must be staring at their backs.

"Oh, nor am I. It's just that at times this furtiveness — the secrecy gets me down . . ."

"We'd better dance," he said and led the way back to the ballroom.

Circling the floor he tried to calm her. "Fenella, we've been over this so often. It's best not to meet . . ."

She looked up at him, her blue eyes filled with tears. "I know. It's just that sometimes . . . sometimes I can't bear . . ."

"I know. It's sheer hell . . . "

"Is it for you? Men are different."

He whirled her round twice. "Of course it's hard for men," he said crossly. "I'm human. It's best for us not to meet, darling."

"But why? We hurt no one . . . "

The music came to an end. There seemed a heavy silence round them.

"Like a drink?" he said abruptly.

She walked with him to the bar. "Tomorrow . . . " she said quietly. "Please Philip. Hilary is going to — to the Adams. I'll be alone. Dan is going to the river — those spares we've been waiting for . . . I'll be alone."

He got the drinks. Took them to her and saw Dan walking towards them, his face taut and anxious. "Look, Fenella," Philip said quickly. "We've discussed this so often. I'm Dan's friend . . . "

"Tomorrow — four o'clock," she whispered. He looked at her and saw she was desperate. He nodded and turned to greet Dan, feeling a Judas.

10

HILARY was in the garden, weeding the strawberry bed, trying to ignore the bored look on Simon's face as the garden *boy* listened to her stumbling words. She felt disheartened, knowing that once she turned her back he would wilfully pull up the strawberry plants and then blandly pretend he had not understood her instructions. Vaguely she heard the telephone bell ringing — and suddenly realized it was for them. Hastily she stood up, brushing off the earth from her hands, hurrying to the house. Fay, she knew, was taking her 'clinic'. As she pushed open the door of the lounge, she stopped dead.

Fay was on the telephone, her voice sharp. "That's impossible. You know it would be dangerous. No, I can't . . . "

There was a desperate note in Fay's voice. Hilary quietly retreated. She had no desire to be caught listening by a half-open door. Fay, these days, was so edgy and suspicious, she would accuse her of 'snooping' and there would be yet another terrible row.

Back to the strawberry bed to find Simon had vanished. Probably gone to lie under a tree and sleep! Stifling a sigh, Hilary began to weed again. The sun beat down mercilessly on to her and despite the big shady hat she wore, her head began to ache. Yet she must do something. You could not sit in a chair all day long, reading.

Fay came briskly round the corner, her starched overall rustling.

"I wondered where you were. I've got to go into Monsimbe. You won't want to come."

Hilary had no desire to go but some inner sense stopped her impulsive words. Obviously this sudden decision to go to Monsimbe was connected with the telephone call and Fay had sounded desperately afraid. It all added up to something — but to what?

"I'd like to come," Hilary said quickly, rising. "I want to get some material to make new undies."

"I'm in a hurry — " Fay began, frowning.

"You've got to change," Hilary pointed out. "I have only to wash my hands." She was wearing a cool green shantung frock that had been clean on that morning.

They drove down the twisting dusty road to Monsimbe in silence. Hilary's head was aching more and more and she knew Fay was in a temper by the way she drove, swinging round corners, skidding madly in the deep dust. At Monsimbe, Fay stopped outside the Royal Hotel.

"I've a lot to do," she said curtly. "Meet you here in two hours."

Hilary hesitated by the side of the car, gazing down the wide dusty street with its few stores and a garage as well as the hotel. She had better buy some material to assuage Fay's suspicions, she decided, so she wandered into one store. One side of it was devoted to Africans — brightly coloured blankets hanging from the roof, a couple of guitars, a bicycle, numerous rolls of gay material, sweets, cigarettes — a colourful hodge-podge of goods round which a dozen Africans stood, laughing and chatting, no one in any hurry. Hilary walked to the other side of the store and smiled at the one-eyed man who limped forward to serve her. He was showing her some crêpe-de-Chine when a familiar voice greeted her.

"Philip — " she turned eagerly, unable to hide her pleasure.

He was smiling down at her. "Don't be extravagant," he teased. "This old devil will rook you if he can — eh, Mike?"

The man grinned. "I have to make a living."

"And a nice fat one it is," Philip laughed. Mike was called to work the cash register and Philip and Hilary were alone for a moment. It was hot and the air rank with the smell of unwashed bodies, but for a second it was heaven to Hilary. She stared up at the good-looking, lean face and wished she could think of something clever to say. If only she could make him see her as a woman . . .

"Enjoy the dance the other night?"

"So much."

There was silence. "You drive yourself in?"

"No, Fay did. She's got some shopping to do."

"Oh . . . " Philip hesitated. He had no desire to run into Fenella just then. The meeting on Tuesday was looming on the horizon and he was wishing for the thousandth time that he had not agreed to it. The trouble was that as soon as he looked into Fenella's eyes, his high resolutions went by the board and he was like clay in her hands. "Well, I must be off . . . "

Hilary felt suddenly desperate. Soon she would be returning to England, never to see him again. "Dan was wondering the other day," she said, her words coming in a little rush, "if you were serious about — about us all going on safari . . . " Dan had mentioned it teasingly, and not in the sense that she wanted to convey now. "I'll be going home soon now and . . . " She stopped, appalled at her own forwardness.

Philip hesitated. The last thing on earth he wanted was to find himself on such intimate terms as a safari with Dan and his wife. Yet he had promised Hilary — and if the child was going back to England, it might be her last chance to have such an experience.

"No, I haven't forgotten," he said slowly. "I'll see what I can organize. We must go before the rains start — that's the main thing." He gave her his rare smile. "I won't forget, Hilary. 'Bye."

"Good-bye."

How empty and desolate the shop seemed when he had gone. She turned back and met Mike's one eye, which was definitely twinkling. She felt her cheeks colour. "I like this pale blue material," she said very firmly.

Two hours was a long time to kill in the small town. She wandered into a dress shop and browsed amongst the dresses, catching fragments of an earnest conversation the plump woman who managed the shop was having on the telephone.

" . . . and I said . . . but that was only the beginning of it. I mean, a girl must have some pride. . . . What? No, he said that, first . . . "

There were no dresses she liked so Hilary successfully resisted temptation. She found it hard to realize that at any moment she would be hearing from the lawyers and would be quite wealthy. What should she do with the money? What should she do with her life?

She walked out of the shop unnoticed, the telephone conversation seeming likely to go on indefinitely, and the full heat of the sun struck her in the street. She lifted her hand to shade her eyes from the glare and at the same moment saw the man.

Instinctively she moved back into the shade of the doorway. Yes — it was the same man. She would know him anywhere. Tall, lean, with a swarthy skin, black hair and those queer grey stony eyes. He was gazing down the street as if looking for someone — and then he turned suddenly and went into the small garage.

"Can I help you?" The plump woman was at Hilary's side, her eyes bright. "Sorry if I kept you waiting."

Hilary turned. Had he seen her? She hoped not. A chill finger seemed to slide down her spine. What was his name? Carlos — Carlos Antunes. The man with the foreign accent and the frightening eyes who had demanded to see Fay, and who had seemed so angry because she was not there.

It was over half an hour later when Hilary at last escaped from the dress shop. She had managed to buy nothing but she had listened to the woman's account of her latest fight with her husband and of what she planned to tell him when she went home that night. "Anyone would think I worked for fun . . . " the woman had spluttered. "And just because the dinner was late last night . . . Men!" she said, her voice expressive. "If they expect us to work and run a house, they must put up with a few delays. It's not easy . . . " She had begun to whine and talk of her bad luck until Hilary was almost desperate to escape.

Hilary walked down to the Royal Hotel — still time to kill. She would have coffee. As she walked into the shabby hotel, she was greeted by Mrs. Adams who waved a white clad hand, her plump chins wobbling as she smiled, and Tallulah Foss — a thin dark girl with slanting eyes and a tongue tipped with acid — as well as Jennifer Hendriks and Burt Wendel. Hilary had to sit at their table and soon everyone was chatting and laughing.

Burt was next to Hilary, looking very handsome with his rather sulky mouth and amused eyes. Hilary often wondered why Anna loved him so deeply — unless it was gratitude — but it was obvious from everything he said, that Burt was very much in love with Anna.

"I'm so glad you're such friends with Anna," he said now. "She needs friends."

"I'm very fond of her. She's a darling," Hilary said warmly.

"She's very sensitive — much more than she shows."

"I know. I wish . . . " Hilary stopped. She did not like to say that she wished her sister was not so hostile to Anna. She looked at her watch. "I mustn't be too long. I'm meeting Fay . . . "

Burt looked startled. "Is she here?" In a few moments, he glanced at his watch and said good-bye to everyone, hurrying out of the lounge as if a devil was at his heels.

Tallulah Foss's eyes were amused as she looked at Hilary. "We always know how to get rid of Burt when we are tired of his company. Just say your sister is coming and he runs."

"But why . . . ?"

There was an uncomfortable silence and Mrs. Adams rushed into the conversation. "Take no notice of Tallulah — she's trying to be funny." She gave the girl an angry glance and then smiled at Hilary. "Are you meeting your sister here?"

"Yes . . . "

At that moment Fay came hurrying in. She looked tired and the bloom of her loveliness seemed tarnished. There were bruised shadows under her eyes, her mouth was pinched. She ordered coffee and sat down with them.

Something made Hilary glance up. A man was standing in the doorway, looking round the room. It was the Portuguese — Carlos Antunes.

Without thought, Hilary caught Fay's arm. "Look, Fay, there's your . . . "

Under the table, Fay's foot hit Hilary's ankle sharply so that it was all she could do not to cry out. She stared at her sister in bewilderment. Fay smiled sweetly. "You were saying . . . " Then something made her turn her head and she saw the man in the doorway. Her whole face seemed to twitch and for a moment she could not speak. "Oh, I see," she said in a strained voice, and turned to Mrs. Adams. "Someone Hilary met on the plane . . . "

Before Hilary could speak, Carlos Antunes had approached the table. He bowed gracefully and spoke to Hilary. "Ah — it is with pleasure that I find you, Mees Hilary. You will introduce me to your friends, no?"

Hilary's throat was dry, her hand lifeless in his. She looked at her sister and met Fay's imploring glance. Hilary could not understand what was happening — all she knew was that Fay was in trouble and was asking for her help. She forced herself to speak, to introduce him, to ignore Tallulah's raised eyebrows, Mrs. Adams's faint withdrawal, the slight tightening of her mouth that expressed disapproval. Carlos drew up a chair and sat chatting for a while. Then he turned to Hilary.

"It is with regret that I must leave you now. I will call another day and pay my respects to Madame, your sister." He gave a little bow to Fay who sat stiffly, her face wearing a set smile. "I am delighted to have had this pleasure of meeting your friends." He smiled at the group.

Tallulah was looking at him with her impish smile. "You are an old friend of Hilary's?"

"W᠁ 'ad the pleasure of making the friendship on the plane," he said slowly. "I am happy to be able to renew that friendship." He rose, bent over the ladies' hands, and then left them.

Tallulah whistled softly. "Some boy friend, Hilary. Watch your step, though. I don't like his eyes."

"Hilary, dear," Mrs. Adams's voice was gently chiding, "I think you should be careful about these sort of friendships. They are similar to those made on ships; you have no chance to study people's background, or get to know them."

Her face flushed, Hilary quickly reassured the older woman. "I don't suppose I shall ever see him again. I was surprised to see him then."

Tallulah leaned forward. "Is it true you're going back to England soon?"

"Yes," Hilary said firmly, her last

doubt banished. She was still shaking inwardly with anger at Fay who had pushed her into such a position. "Yes, I am."

"Look — Ned and I are going to spend a few days with the Morgans and I wondered if you'd care to come too. They live in a Game Reserve and I know you're interested in wild life. It would be quite an experience."

Fay spoke abruptly. "Hilary's scared — I think she'd hate it."

Hilary's cheeks were hot. "I'd love to, thanks, Tallulah." She looked at Fay defiantly. "I'm getting used to animals now."

Tallulah told her they would call for her and when to be ready. "We'll go on Saturday and be back the following Thursday. You've met them, Hilary, I think. They have a small boy called Jackie."

"I remember," Hilary said and deliberately turned her head to look at her sister. But Fay did not seem to mind; she merely smiled and shrugged.

It was on the way home that Hilary lost her temper.

"It was all a put-up plot, wasn't it?" she asked, her voice shaking. "You planned to make me introduce that man as a friend of mine."

Fay scowled at the road ahead. "It was Carlos's idea."

"But you backed him up. How dared you — I . . . I wouldn't be seen dead with a man like that. I hate to think what Mrs. Adams thought . . . "

"She's got an unpleasant mind, anyhow. It didn't hurt you and it may have helped me — " Fay swung round the corner, the car skidding in the dust. She braked violently as a couple of monkeys raced across the road, chattering and gazing vindictively at the car.

"But HOW can it help you? Why do you know such a person, Fay? He's dangerous . . . "

Fay laughed. "You're telling me . . ."

"But why . . . "

She wanted to ask Fay so much yet she could not. It must have been Carlos who telephoned — who made Fay sound so desperate. What was it she had said on the telephone? "*That's impossible. You know it would be dangerous.*"

211

Yet if she told Fay that, Fay would know she had overheard the telephone conversation. She would accuse her of 'snooping', Fay's favourite expression, and Hilary would have less chance than ever of helping her. Hilary was certain that Fay was afraid of Carlos — and that she had to do what Carlos said. What did it mean? Blackmail?

Hilary shuddered. She would hate to be at the mercy of such a man.

Fay spoke curtly. "I wish you'd mind your own damned business. I never asked you to come out here and you're nothing but a nuisance. I don't need your help and I wish you'd stop interfering. It's my life and . . . "

"But you're afraid of him — " Hilary blurted out.

Fay's mouth was a thin line. "I can cope. Just keep out of this." As the car jerked to a standstill outside the house, Fay turned her head, her face distorted with anger. "I wish to God you'd never come out — I wish you'd go home."

Before Hilary could answer, Dan came out of the house. There was an odd look on his face. "Philip has just telephoned," he told them. "He's laying on a safari for Hilary in three weeks' time. Won't that be jolly?" he added sarcastically.

Fay climbed out of the car. "It should be quite an experience for Hilary," she said coldly.

"I may not be here — in three weeks' time," Hilary said, her voice desperate.

Dan's hand was warm on hers as he helped her out of the car. He smiled.

"You must be, Hilary. It's an experience you must not miss."

11

THE Morgans' was a roomy white-painted mud and wattle house with a veranda running right round and serving to keep the rooms cool. The Morgans, a young couple with one child, Jackie, welcomed Hilary warmly.

"When Tallulah suggested you join them, we thought it a wonderful plan," Nancy Morgan said, leading the way to an airy cool bedroom. "Have you really got to go back to England? Wouldn't you rather stay out here?" She was a thin girl with straight black hair and friendly eyes. "Jock is always saying he will take me to England one day but we never save enough money." She laughed cheerfully. "I don't know that I want to go to England, really. From all I hear of it, it rains the whole time and the sun never shines."

"Oh, it does," Hilary said quickly. "We have terrific heat waves." She had discovered that living abroad had made her fiercely patriotic, and the slightest suggestion of criticism of England — be it the weather, politics, living conditions or the people — made her get all 'hot and bothered' in their defence.

The Morgans were a pleasant couple and Tallulah and Ned full of fun, and it was a pleasant few days for Hilary.

She loved the long drives by Jock's side in his Rover, his gun handy, as they took her mile after mile through the Reserve, telling her of the old days before the Reserves were started, when the game was killed wantonly and without reason, and how some of the animals had almost been wiped out.

"But now that they are protected, things are much better." He told her how the Reserves attracted tourists. " — and tourists bring money into the country."

He told her a lot about poaching. "Dan will know all about that," he added. "It's one of our outsize headaches. You see, you can get a license for shooting but you're only allowed to kill so many animals. Some people are greedy killers

— others want the skins or the ivory. Not that many poachers get away with it — we have a very excellent espionage system — we put our spies in the poachers' camp and soon pick 'em up," he said grimly. "The thing is, people will do anything for money. Lots of game is shot just for biltong — know what that is?" He described how the animals were cut and sliced into strips of meat, these to be hung in the sunshine for a certain length of time. "It's an acquired taste. I like biltong — Nancy loathes it. It's actually dried raw meat and a man can live on it for a long time. It's real old Boer food."

He showed her herds of giraffe feeding off tall trees, their long necks out-stretched. He showed her the hippo pool; and she stared amazed at the groups of rock-like prehistoric looking creatures, with their bright eyes and absurdly comic babies. He showed her a hyena and as it made off, it gave a cry that sent a shiver down her spine. He showed her a family — Father lion, his wife and several cubs.

Jock and Hilary sat quietly in the Rover watching the family at play. At first she had not found it easy to make them out — the mane of the lion blending with the thorn bushes, but then she saw the amber eyes, staring unblinkingly at the car. How grim the lion looked, she thought with a shudder, and wondered if this looking at wild animals was as dangerous as it felt. Look at those two deep channels that run from the corner of the eyes down to the turned-down mouth — what mighty shoulders. The lion stood up, stretching himself, turning, like an actor on the stage making sure his audience did not miss a single good feature. What enormous paws . . . And then, as they watched, the lion lay down on his back and the cubs began to climb all over him, making delighted sounds, playing with him, nipping him. And then, just like an irate father who suddenly loses patience, the lion sat up suddenly, tumbling the cubs to the ground, giving one of them a smart cuff on the face and stalking off, to sit alone, his back turned, aloof, indifferent, while the lioness began licking the cubs vigorously as if to say: Now, look how grubby your father has made you!

Jock was watching Hilary's rapt face. "Rather sweet, eh?"

She turned glowing eyes. "They're so human," she whispered.

He grinned and drove on. Later they camped in the shade of some high rocks and the cookboy they had with them grilled Tommy-meat. Jock and Hilary were alone and she got him talking about the country.

"Why is it worth poaching?" she wanted to know.

He told her that the zebra is wanted for his beautiful coat, the wildebeeste for his tail, the giraffe for his skin, tail and mane.

"Buck are shot for meat and we game wardens close our eyes to this as folks must live, but any large scale shooting in order to get meat for biltong is illegal so we clamp down on that. Lion grease fetches a very high price from witch doctors and dandies — " he laughed at her face. "I mean it! Then of course there are always poachers for ivory, and the slaughter of elephants that used to take place was almost unbelievable."

Sitting in the blessed shade, Hilary

asked him if he liked the life.

"It's the only life — " he stretched his long powerfully-muscled arms over his head. "Sometimes I wonder, though, if it is a good life for Nancy and Jackie." He sighed. "It's what I've been trained to do. I can't imagine any other kind of life."

Hilary thought of the six-foot wire fence round the garden of the house, of the gates with their double locks in case Jackie, now four and growing more skilful every day, should try to open one. She thought of the Reserve which surrounded the house — where wild animals walked unmolested, not shut in behind wire but leading normal lives as they might in the jungle.

"Isn't it dangerous living with lions and elephants?" she said a little timidly, fearing his laughter, thinking of Tallulah's contempt for her when she had said, rather nervously, that she hoped no lion would jump in her open window.

Jock broke off a long blade of grass and chewed it. "The lion is not a man-eater unless he is wounded and unable to kill. You see, lions are very slow in comparison with the animals they hunt so that when a lion is old or wounded, he gets hungry and seeks an easy prey. That's when he makes off with children or goats. Normally, though, a lion will leave you alone. So long as people behave themselves in the Reserves it seems as though lions do not connect cars with man. They will come quite close and walk round a car, looking at it curiously. Elephants are different — but even then they will only charge if provoked. There is no danger at all if you drive carefully and quietly. In the years I've been here, I've never heard of an accident."

Hilary relaxed a little. She was ashamed of her own fears but conscious that all the time she sat in the shade of these rocks, her body was tense with fear. Jock seemed so sure of himself and yet she kept wondering if some animal would creep up behind.

"A leopard," Jock went on, "is far more dangerous than a lion. He is a killer. He likes guinea fowl and poultry and takes his game into trees where he hides them and eats them at leisure. You mustn't forget that hyenas and wild dogs are always on the look-out for game that has been killed. Leopards, especially when wounded, are far more dangerous than lions." He repeated: "You know it's a strange position. Leopards are the farmer's foe for they kill his poultry, so every farmer is entitled to kill leopards; on the other hand leopards kill baboons. Now baboons are a much greater enemy of the farmer than leopards." He smiled. "Sounds odd, doesn't it? You see, baboons can do more harm in a field of growing maize or coffee than a herd of elephants could, so you see the farmer is in a quandary. He doesn't want to lose his poultry, but it's even worse to lose a crop of maize or coffee. The leopard also kills bush pigs and wild dogs, so in that he helps the farmer as well. It's some problem. Then there is another point. A leopard skin is worth anything from ten pounds to twenty pounds so you can see how poachers make a good thing out of killing 'em — and that is the last thing the farmer wants to encourage."

"What is the solution?" Hilary asked, stifling a yawn; not because she was bored — far from it, she loved being told these things: the sort of information that Fay took it for granted she should know; but the day was very hot and she had eaten too well.

Jock filled his pipe. "It's rather clever. You are allowed to shoot a leopard but you must report it to the Game Warden; he then pays for the skin and keeps the skin for the Crown. That way we keep a check on the leopards killed and it stops undisciplined shooting."

His voice sounded farther and farther away. She awoke with a jerk to find herself alone. She sat upright. The sun had moved and they were no longer in the shade. She jumped to her feet. She could not see the Rover or any sign of Jock. Overwhelming panic seized her. How still it was! She looked over her shoulder — was a snake now creeping along the branch overhead, waiting to drop? Was a leopard watching her from the safety of the caves above?

She felt she could not wait to be attacked. She stumbled forward and found a faint track — surely those were signs of tyre treads? The sun blazed down — there were waves of heat coming up from the ground. Under the thorn trees, the grass was waist high. She would not dare to walk in there because of the snakes.

Where was Jock? Fear rose in her throat . . .

And then she heard the Rover. It appeared between the thorn trees, backing carefully down the narrow track. She was breathless with relief when Jock reached her.

"I thought you'd gone off and forgotten me — "

He was looking grim. "I only left you for a second. One of the *boys* brought me news of some poachers and I fetched the Rover after I had sent them off. Hop in — I'm going to catch them if I can."

They drove as fast as they could between the low spreading branches of the trees, turning sharply to avoid a tall ant hill, lurching round an old twisted baobab whose branches looked like a witch's arms stretched out to grab sacrifices. They could see a distant aloof mountain but here all was yellow sand with every bush and tree covered with spikes and thorns. Hilary clung to the side of the Rover which bucked and jumped over the uneven ground like a bronco not yet broken. She felt for the first time the thrill, the attraction of this bush veldt; where every bush might hide elephant or rhino; where the zebra could be seen loping across the bald yellow spaces between the trees and the buck leapt away in terror as the Rover roared by.

This is the life, Jock had said. And so had Dan. But was it also the life for their wives? Should men like these be dedicated to their work, like priests? Was it right to ask a woman to share such an existence? For a woman's life must necessarily be different. Tied to her house, she would not feel the pull of the fascinating country, she would only see the disadvantages. Yet Hilary knew that if Philip had asked her to share his life — to live in a lonely animal-haunted place like the Morgans — she would have fallen over herself with haste to accept. If you loved a man . . .

The Rover jerked to a standstill. Jock pointed out some black shapes twisting and turning in the sky. "Vultures," he said shortly. "They'll lead us to the poachers. It's amazing how soon they smell blood."

They drove on more slowly and stopped again as one of Jock's scouts stepped out from beneath a thorn tree, his hand raised. Jock listened to what he had to say and then turned, frowning, to Hilary.

"Look — I don't like to leave you alone in the Rover. Think you can walk with us?"

"Oh yes," she said very quickly. "Please don't leave me."

He was still frowning, hesitating. "It may not be a pretty sight . . . "

"I needn't look," she said, even more quickly.

He grinned. "Okay. Keep close behind me and the *boy* will follow you. You'll be perfectly safe."

They walked through waist deep grass, Hilary keeping her fingers crossed and praying she would not step on a snake. The daylight was green here because the sun could not get through the closely matted branches overhead. They walked fast, the perspiration pouring off her, until her shirt was soaked. She was thankful for the khaki slacks Tallulah had lent her, glad her legs were not bare as they brushed past thorn bushes.

Suddenly Jock halted her with a warning hand. They could see straight ahead — an open glade of short green grass. As they stood there, she focused her eyes and saw that there were no longer just the three of them. Two other boys were there, wearing their khaki shorts and shirts and pillbox hats. They were all looking expectantly towards Jock. He stood — hand upraised warningly.

Suddenly there was a drumming sound, and the next moment across the open glade came a herd of wildebeeste, running madly, their heavy bodies disturbing the air and throwing off a strange musky scent, as their hoofs beat on the ground.

Hilary instinctively ducked as there was a whining hum like that of a mosquito — and one of the animals faltered, ran a little farther and then collapsed, his legs seeming to crumple under him. He lay, jerking and kicking and Hilary caught her breath with pity. One moment so big and healthy, so full of vigorous life, and now collapsed and inert. Jock's hand was still held up warningly and even as they waited, a dozen Africans came running.

It was like a scene out of the past; these dozen Africans loping along, with skins tied round their waists and their bare shoulders gleaming wetly in the bright light, it might have been a scene from an old film; each one holding in his hand a long powerful bow, and a long quiver of arrows slung round his neck. As they reached the dead wildebeeste one African stooped and with a quick slash of his knife, cut off the tail — he already had two tails attached to his belt, swinging, as he ran. Another African was cutting out the steel-pointed arrow from the side of the beast — yet a third had slashed the animal's throat with a quick decisive movement.

At that moment, Jock stepped forward and spoke loudly. The dozen Africans swung round, their faces almost comical in their dismay. Jock's *boys* moved in, their guns at the ready, their faces cold.

★ ★ ★

The Rover jolted back to the Morgans' house with a full complement — six Africans in the back — with the rest of the prisoners left behind with a guard. Jock drove fast, the Rover jolting and jerking like a wild thing. Gone was Hilary's sleepiness. Her whole body tingled — not with excitement but with a quiet confidence. She had walked through the jungle and not been afraid! She smiled at Jock and he grinned back.

"You have quite a time," she teased.

"Oh yes, vet, doctor and policeman, that's me," he chuckled. "The worst time is when the Africans trap the animals and I have to shoot 'em 'cos I can't save 'em." He had sobered, his face grave. "Shooting is clean killing — what I can't bear is the animals being trapped and left to die slowly."

Hilary shuddered. "Do they do it much?"

"The whole time, my girl. Pits for them to fall in — stakes to be impaled on — poisoned meat-traps . . ." He shivered. "That part of my job gets me down."

Back at the house, Hilary went in alone

as Jock had to arrange to fetch the other prisoners and to arrange transport for the lot to go to the nearest charge office.

Tallulah and Nancy were having tea — they looked up smiling. Jackie came running, his cheeks flushed, his voice fretful.

"I don't know what's wrong with Jackie," Nancy sighed wearily. "He's so cross all the time."

That night Jackie cried a great deal. In the morning his mother said she wished she hadn't broken their only thermometer. Jackie, small, blond and tough, tossed and turned in bed, demanding attention and complaining bitterly if he didn't get it. Tallulah and Hilary sat in the bright white-walled lounge, looking out of the window at the high wire fence, carefully moving their legs and nylons from the friendly paws of Mopsy, the baby leopard Jock had found starving as a tiny cub, and had tamed.

Mopsy was a lovable beast — according to Jock — but very playful. Still only small, her paws had an amazing strength and if she unleashed her claws she could rip nylons to pieces. Hilary had stroked her timidly and had been rather touched when Mopsy came to lean against her, making a sound very similar to a cat's purring when her head was scratched. At the same time, she felt far from comfortable when Mopsy was in the room and ventured to say something of the sort to Tallulah. To her surprise, Tallulah had agreed.

"It's crazy to rear these wild animals. Jock must be mad," she said almost crossly. "What's going to happen when this beast is fully grown? You can never trust them. She'll have to be shot or sent to a zoo. I think the former is preferable. I don't know how Nancy stands the life here. Ours is bad enough, but at least when we go on safari, we meet new faces."

That evening Jackie was worse, he was slightly delirious, and the aspirin they gave him did not seem to lower his obvious temperature. Nancy looked up from bending over the bed, her face worried.

"Jock, I think we should get him to a doctor . . ."

Jock ran his hand wildly through his short blond hair. "It's seventy miles. Do you think he should be moved?"

Tallulah suggested: "Why not ring the doctor and tell him Jackie's symptoms."

Nancy half-groaned. "Everyone will listen in on the party line and later ring up to give me good advice. But it might be an idea."

She came back from the telephone, her face drawn and white. "He seems to think we should get Jackie into hospital. He suggests we leave at dawn . . . " She hesitated and looked at her guests.

Ned, who had been looking through Jock's collection of coloured slides, looked up. "Don't worry about us, Nancy, we'll get off home at dawn, too."

Nancy looked as if she could cry. "We so seldom get visitors and now we are driving you away."

Ned got up and put his arm clumsily round her. "We'll come down again and bring Hilary with us eh?" He grinned at his wife and Hilary. "We've had a whale of a time — I know Hilary has, I can see it bubbling out of her, all the things she'll have to tell the old folks at home." He chuckled. "Don't worry, Nancy. Babies always get one in a panic — that's why Tallulah and I don't want to start a family yet. You take him to the hospital and he'll be fit as a flea in two days."

So next morning when the sky was still pearly grey and the sun only a golden whisper on the horizon, the two Rovers set off; Jock driving Nancy, whose white strained face was bent over the flushed sleeping Jackie, and making for the hospital at Genmoe; Tallulah and Hilary turning off for Monsimbe.

It was lunch time before they reached the town so they stopped at the hotel to eat and then drove Hilary home. Both Ned and Tallulah said they'd prefer not to stop if Hilary understood and she waved them good-bye from the veranda. As she went into the house, Fay came out of the bedroom.

She did not look very pleased to see Hilary. "I thought you weren't coming back until Thursday," she said ungraciously. "This is only Tuesday."

Hilary explained. "I had a wonderful time," she finished, her eyes glowing, all ready to tell Fay about it.

Fay was not interested, nor very concerned about Jackie. "Nancy flaps over every ache and pain that child has," she said rather scornfully. "You've had lunch, of course. Like a cup of coffee? I'm making myself some."

Hilary said she would and went off to wash the dust off her face and brush her hair vigorously. She would have preferred tea but had not liked to say so. Fay had a 'thing' about her coffee but Hilary found it very bitter.

It was exceptionally bitter that day and when Fay went out of the room for a moment, Hilary hastily tipped half of the cup's contents out of the open window and so only had half a cupful to struggle through. She went to change her dress and caught herself in an overwhelming yawn.

"Why don't you have a rest?" Fay suggested from the doorway. "You must be tired. It's quite a journey from the Morgans and Ned is a tiring driver." Her sympathetic voice surprised Hilary and she looked round. Fay was smiling at her. "Did I sound very snappy about

Nancy?" Fay went on, "but we've all suffered from her mother-fixation. She thinks Jackie is dying, and panics if he gets a cold." She leaned against the doorpost. "You enjoyed yourself?"

Hilary yawned and stretched luxuriously. "Marvellous. Oh, Fay, I saw such a lot of game. Lions — even elephants in the distance. They've got a baby leop . . ." the word vanished in another yawn. "I was out with Jock and we caught poachers . . ."

"You what?" Fay said sharply.

Hilary was too busy yawning to notice Fay's face. "We caught poachers . . ." She yawned again. "It was thrilling, like a film. We waited and along came a great herd of wildebeeste — there was a shot . . ." Yawn. "And one fell, poor thing. Then a crowd of Africans came out, all with bows and arrows. Bows — and arrows, Fay — just like olden times. Oh . . ." She yawned again. "I am tired."

Fay's face was pinched and white. "Did they get the *boys*?"

"Oh yes, Jock arrested twelve of them."

"Did they . . . talk?"

In the middle of a yawn, Hilary looked at her. "Talk?"

Fay turned away. "Of course you wouldn't know. Have a good sleep and tell me all about it later."

It was a weird kind of sleep. Hilary felt as if she was sinking — sinking into a deep pit with a great smothering blanket shutting out the air. She struggled awake, only to find her eyes glued shut and her body unable to move, she fell asleep again, struggling to stay awake.

And then she awoke. And was completely and lucidly awake. She lay very still under the thin sheet and a little breeze rippled through the open window and, with a slight creak her bedroom door opened. It led to Fay's room and, as if from a distance, there came voices.

Philip's.

Instantly Hilary was on her feet, combing her hair, her hand shaking as she found her powder puff, going to the cupboard for a dress. She had so much to tell Philip. And then quite clearly — she heard Philip say:

"You know I love you, Fenella. I've told you often enough."

Hilary stood still, shocked and disbelieving her own ears.

Philip spoke again, slowly. "I love you . . . "

It was Fay who spoke next, quickly. "Just a moment." And Hilary could hear her heels on the polished floor, going clack-clack.

Hilary had never moved so fast in all her life as she jumped into bed, pulling up the sheet and closing her eyes. The clack-clack of the high heels came closer — then there was a pause as if Fay was looking into the room and then there was a gentle click as the door closed. Slowly Hilary relaxed, opening her eyes, staring at the ceiling. Her mouth felt thick and unpleasant and her head throbbed painfully.

Again and again, she heard the words. 'I love you — I love you.' The most terrible desolation seized her. Philip loved Fay, even though she was married. And if Philip was in love with Fay, he would never, never, never fall in love with Fay's unattractive young sister. That was for sure. So that even if Philip DID get over his love for Fay, there was no hope for

236

her, Hilary realized.

She turned her face into the pillow and felt the burning tears well up in her eyes. It had been a dream. She should have realized that. If only her head didn't throb so — her heart ache so badly. How did you give up a dream — even when you had to?

12

THE day they heard from the solicitor that the will had been proved, marked a peak in Hilary's life. Ever since the day she had awakened from what she realized must have been a drugged sleep, and had heard Philip tell Fay that he loved her, she had moved automatically as in a cloud of misery. She believed no one knew or noticed; she made every effort to be the same, not to let it affect her feeling for Fay but, of course, it did.

She would catch herself watching Fay's face; would listen to the constant bickering and wonder if Dan knew that Fay was in love with his best friend; would wonder again and again why a man like Philip had to fall in love with a married woman.

They saw quite a lot of Philip, both at parties and when he came to see Dan. He was always the same, acting somewhat like a benevolent head-master

238

towards Hilary; looking quickly at Fay, and even more quickly away again as if afraid to trust himself.

It was like a gnawing cancer inside her — the knowledge that he loved Fay. Hilary found herself counting the days to the safari that had been planned, because she knew that, once that was over, she must get away. If not back to England, then to some other part of Africa.

The will was the spark to set off Fay's anger.

"It's not fair," she raged. "Five thousand for you, Hilary, while I get a miserable two thousand. What good is two thousand?" she demanded scornfully, two flags of anger blazing in her cheeks. "And I don't see why you should get the income from ten thousand while I . . . "

Hilary, writhing silently, was stung to reply: "Don't forget you get half of that when I marry."

Fay looked startled — then smiled sarcastically. "So I suppose I'll have to find you a husband. Pity Philip didn't fall for you — he's the only eligible male here."

The taunt — for surely it was nothing else? — stung.

"If I die," Hilary said, "then you'll get the lot."

Fay stared at her for a moment and her face grew thoughtful. "Yes — if you die . . ." And then, with typical Fay inconsistency, her face changed and she caught Hilary's hand. "Darling — I couldn't bear it if you died. I'd rather not have the money. No, it's a husband I must find you." She was smiling now, teasing.

"I don't know that I want to get married," Hilary said slowly.

Fay laughed outright. "Oh, don't talk tripe, darling. Every woman wants a husband."

But despite Fay's temporary change of mood, there was still an uncomfortable undercurrent in the household. It worried and alarmed Hilary. The telephone, for one thing. Often in the evening, as they sat having a 'sundowner' their number would be called and Dan would go. He would come back, puzzled.

"I don't know who it was — they rang off as soon as I spoke."

And Hilary would see Fay's knuckles whiten, the backs of her hands go taut as she clenched her fists. She would feel, with Fay, the tension of the moment.

Sometimes during the day, the same thing would happen. If Hilary answered, there would be an expectant hush. She knew it was absurd to let it worry her but it was as though someone was watching and threatening them.

Fay, too, went about as if under some terrific strain. She snapped everyone's head off, was always complaining about the servants — screaming at them in their own language; and old Petrus with his grizzled hair and his 'Uncle Tom' look, would shrink away, half lifting one hand as if to protect himself.

Then strange things happened; things that Hilary might not have noticed normally but that now, being so conscious of Fay's tension, she could not fail to see. Several times Fay had driven Carl and Petrus to Monsimbe, promising to bring them back with her, only to return alone, complaining that they had not met her at the promised time. Then she would send Simon, the garden *boy*, with the odd face and the scornful eyes, to get them. And in a while, there would be an alarm on the telephone. Fire! . . .

Dan, if he was around, would race off with every *boy* he could find. Or else he would have to be traced and given a message. And Fay's face would grow thin and pointed, her cheeks flushed, her eyes very bright, and she would sit, perched uncomfortably on the edge of a chair, waiting.

One day, alone with Dan, Hilary asked tentatively, "Aren't there being an awful lot of fires, Dan? Is it the dry season?"

The night before there had been a terrible storm — terrific claps of thunder cracking overhead and rumbling into the distance, and, at the same time, frightening forks of lightning zig-zagging against the blue-black sky.

Dan was filling his pipe. He grunted and looked up, "No — if I tell you something, keep it under your hat." He looked at her with shrewd eyes. "We're not letting this get about but those fires are deliberate."

A cold shiver slid down her back. "But why?"

242

"To decoy us away. You see, even though we guess they're faked, we daren't risk ignoring the calls, for they might not be. Meantime we all go off to scotch the fire and what happens?" He lifted his pipe and waved it at her. "Poachers step in."

Hilary sat upright. "Here? I didn't think you had them here. Jock said . . . "

Dan grinned. "Jock has only one idea, his beloved Reserve. We have our poaching problems here, too. It's no casual business, either. The whole thing is too well organized." He leaned forward. "They slaughtered fifty elephants the other day when we were called away to the fire by the Peak."

"Oh no . . . "

"Quite a good haul of ivory that. Well worth the risk."

"But — but what are you doing about it?"

He shrugged. "Philip has some idea he can trap them." He looked grim. "I'm sorry for the gang if he does. It's a pretty serious crime, you know. Another point often overlooked is that of wounding the animals. No hunter would leave a wounded animal — he's GOT to find that animal and kill it, but poachers have no time to waste tracking wounded animals."

Hilary's eyes were bright with interest. "To put the poor thing out of its agony?"

Dan smiled. "Well, there's that side of it, of course, but also because a wounded animal is a very real danger. He turns killer and then we really have fun. It can take us months to track him down — meantime he can kill dozens of children and women."

Hilary shuddered. She looked up and saw Fay in the doorway, watching them, an odd look on her face.

"I've just been admiring your garden," Fay said sweetly, "or what there is of it. Seems we had visitors last night. Have you seen the spoor, Dan?"

Dan stood up, pushing his chair away from the table, Samson close at hand.

"I heard Samson growling in the night but I was too darned tired to care."

"So nice for us," Fay said with acid sweetness. "We might have been killed while you blissfully snored . . . "

They followed her outside. There

— bang in the middle of Hilary's cherished strawberry bed were deep broad marks — a small hedge of flowering shrubs had been trampled on — a fence knocked down.

Simon stood there. "*Tembo, bwana,*" he said.

Dan was frowning. "I've never known them come up to the house before. Don't go wandering off, Hilary," he said curtly. "And don't go out in the car alone at the moment."

"And what about me?" Fay asked, "or don't you care?"

Dan swung round and for a moment his face was so vulnerable that Hilary wanted to run away, she felt embarrassed because he had shown so clearly what Fay meant to him.

"Don't be a bloody fool," he snapped, "you know how to take care of yourself." He swung away. "I'll let Philip know this — there may be a rogue elephant amongst them and the village down the bill is so bloody exposed . . . "

"What does *Tembo* mean?" Hilary asked.

Fay looked at her with amusement.

245

"Elephant, of course."

Hilary shivered. "You mean — you mean elephants walked round our house last night? Why, they might . . . "

"Might have knocked one of the walls down," Fay finished for her, her mouth twisted with amusement. "Sure they might — and rolled on us until we were flat as pancakes. You heard what Dan said — you'd better stay put, Hilary. I'm going into town."

"But . . . " Hilary began and bit off the sentence. She sat alone in the house, looking out of the window and wondering what she would do if a huge elephant loomed up outside the door. It was a very ramshackle building — she did not think it would stand up to an angry elephant.

She rang Anna and found, to her comfort, that to Anna it was an every-day occurrence.

"Nothing at all to worry about. Fay could have told you that. Dan's right of course, don't go wandering out of the garden or in the car alone. There should be two of you, one with a gun. It's probably one of the elephants from the Reserve looking for water. There is

246

something of a drought."

"But aren't elephants dangerous?"

"Only when they are angered. I wouldn't care to run into a herd if I was alone in the car," Anna admitted. "But if I saw one in the garden, I'd just lie low and keep very quiet. It wouldn't hurt you."

"I'll take your word for it," Hilary tried to laugh.

It was a relief when Fay came home though Hilary tried to hide it. Fay seemed very silent and it was after Dan had gone that she gave Hilary a queer considering look.

"Would you like to see a witch doctor?"

The question took Hilary by surprise. "Why — yes . . . "

"I'm seeing one this afternoon. We need rain badly and I promised to see if I could fix it," Fay said as casually as if she had announced she was going to buy a new hat, "We'll go to his kraal this afternoon."

Hilary's mouth was dry. "The ele-phant . . . "

Fay looked at her with contempt.

"We'll take the Mauser with us and you're supposed to be a wonderful shot."

"But where would I shoot an elephant?" Despite every effort, Hilary's voice shook.

Fay smiled. "Where the trunk meets his forehead — that's the vital spot. But I doubt if we will see him — or them, for elephants rarely travel alone. The one who came up here may have been more adventurous or thirsty than the others."

They set off in the car, the gun by Hilary's hand. She was trembling so much she wondered Fay could not see. How ramshackle and frail the car looked! Her mouth was dry as Fay drove quickly down the track towards Monsimbe, then turned off on to what was little more than two dried ruts, right through the thorn bushes. By now, Hilary was so accustomed to seeing buck leaping over bushes, or a giraffe in the distance, and occasionally a slinking wild dog, that she rarely got excited, but today she sat, tense with fear, expecting to see a huge elephant straddling the path at any moment.

It was a relief to reach a native village, to drive through, bumping over stones and ruts, to see the small black piccaninnies come running out with their distended tummies and their gleaming teeth and bright excited eyes, to see the women bending over black pots that were cooking on wood fires, to see the odd man lounging on the grass, whittling away at something in his hand. They drove on until they reached a solitary hut.

Fay got out and Hilary had to follow her. Outside the hut, Fay stopped and spoke, haughty — imperious. In a moment, something stirred inside and a man came out, crouching to get through the low entrance.

Hilary caught a whiff of awful stench and she held her breath as she stared in amazement and some dismay. He was a tall thin African, emaciated to the point of resembling a skeleton, his eyes deeply sunk in dark sockets in a high-boned shiny face. Round his waist was twisted a skin belt and from this dangled skulls. Hilary hardly dared glance at them, wondering if they were animal or human. There were bones strung round his shoulders; round his neck and arms were necklaces of animal teeth. He had a kaross which looked as if it was made of a monkey skin slung over one shoulder. His eyes were slits and the whites of them yellowish. His lips curled back and his teeth were mostly rotten black stumps. He stared at them silently and Hilary had to conquer a strong desire to turn and run to the car. Did Fay know what she was doing? What would Dan say if he knew they were alone with a witch doctor?

And then the witch doctor spoke, his voice guttural, the words jumping out with little explosive sounds. He came closer and they could smell his foul breath.

Fay was smiling. She began to talk, her voice still imperious. Hilary knew a warm rush of admiration for her. Fay was afraid of nothing.

They seemed to talk for hours. And then the witch doctor took a small leather bag from his shoulder and opened it. He had a handful of shiny polished bones which he turned over and over in his hand, mumbling something, his eyes fixed on Fay. Abruptly he stopped and threw the bones on the ground

— watching them as they fell. He looked up, his lips curling back from his gums, as he said something.

Fay plunged her hand in her pocket and gave him a bottle of brown liquid and a handful of silver. She turned to Hilary and spoke curtly. "Let's go."

Hilary was only too willing. They had been bumping over the track for some time before Fay spoke. "What did you think of him?"

Hilary shuddered. "He stank. You don't seriously believe he has any power?"

Fay gave her a curious look. "You'd be surprised how often things they foretell come true."

"Can he send rain?" Hilary said sarcastically.

Fay laughed. "He's promised to . . . You know, you can laugh if you like but it often works. I don't know if they're lucky or what, but very often if you get a witch doctor who knows his job, rain does follow. He told me . . . " her voice lilted, "that I would get my heart's desire soon."

Hilary turned and stared. "Why, I

do believe you are serious?" she said wonderingly. "What is your heart's desire?"

Fay shrugged, giving all her attention for a moment to the car. "Can't you guess?" she said cryptically.

"But seriously, Fay, I wouldn't have thought you would go in for fortune tellers and . . . "

Fay gave her a quick amused glance. "Why not, if it brightens life a little? At least it gives one some hope that this ghastly deadlock will soon end."

Hilary sat very still, trying to puzzle it out. Something made her hesitate to ask Fay what she meant by 'ghastly deadlock'. Could Fay's 'heart's desire' be that Dan give her a divorce so that she could be free to marry Philip?

As the car bumped and rattled, she realized that she had forgotten all about the rogue elephant. Her anxiety for Fay was too great. Fay was obviously frightened of Carlos, was undergoing some sort of strain, and now she admitted that she believed in witch doctors. What did it all mean?

13

IT seemed to Hilary that she must do something about her fears for Fay. So, feeling a little guilty because it rather resembled the 'snooping' Fay so often accused her of doing, Hilary began to ask questions, or more accurately, to invite remarks.

Tallulah of the candid nature and acid-tipped tongue, told her most. Hilary was dismayed to find that Fay was not generally liked.

"She's good fun and all that," Tallulah had said, "but — but there's something odd about her. It may be her eyes, they have a queer look — and then — then she's so utterly ruthless, and honestly, Hilary, it sounds nasty to say it, but she has no scruples, has she?"

Of course it was true. It was what their father had meant when he said Fay was 'amoral'.

Tallulah told Hilary something that shocked her even more. It seemed that

Fay had had violent love affairs with practically every man in the neighbourhood.

"It's as if she's burned up by some need to possess people — to have them as her slaves. Even my husband fell heavily for her," Tallulah added ruefully.

"But you were married when you came here."

Tallulah laughed. "Would that worry our sweet Fay? Luckily she soon got tired of him," she finished bitterly.

"And Anna's husband? Is that why Fay hates Anna so much?"

"Oh no — that was totally different." Tallulah looked wickedly gleeful. "He snubbed Fay right, left and centre. I think he was the first man to repulse her. He had no time for her and let her, and everyone else, know it. I don't know if I am right but I think it did something to Fay. Made her worse than she might have been. I don't think she'll ever forgive him for it and then when he arrived with Anna for a wife — well, Fay saw that as a deliberate insult."

Mrs. Adams also talked when she saw that Hilary was not going to be upset.

"My dear, if only you could persuade Dan to take her home for a year or even less," she said, her plump face concerned. "I'm sure this place has had an adverse influence on your sister. She has changed so . . . " She tch-tch-ed a little. "You know this sort of life doesn't suit everyone — some natures can't stand up to it." She looked keenly at Hilary's worried face. "You, my dear, have lost your youthful bloom. You're not happy here?"

Hilary moved her hands vaguely. "Not very," she admitted. "I'm used to an active life and . . . "

Mrs. Adams nodded. "I know, dear, you don't need to tell *me*. Dan is a dear patient man but I think, sometimes, a little *too* patient."

Hilary coloured and changed the subject. She did not wish to discuss Fay's matrimonial troubles with anyone.

She tried to sort it out. Surely it just meant that Fay was a very attractive girl with a strong personality, cooped up in a life she hated; needing an outlet for her talents; needing to meet people; needing a fuller life altogether. Well, Fay could have her holiday in England. She had the money, and Hilary thought, she would help her. Surely if Dan knew how Fay needed a change, he would agree?

But Dan, oddly enough, did not agree. Hilary had managed to get him to herself and to suggest that it would be lovely if Fay could go home with her for a few months. An oddly stubborn look came over Dan's face. "This is her home."

"Of course . . . I didn't mean . . . " Hilary stumbled, annoyed with herself for having started so tactlessly. "I thought the voyage home — we might fly to Beira and go home by sea and . . . I mean go to England by sea and see some friends and . . . "

"Has Fay put you up to this?" Dan asked stiffly.

"Oh no," Hilary said very quickly. "It was my own idea. I didn't want to suggest it if you couldn't spare her."

Dan's mouth tightened. "That's just it," he said. "I couldn't spare her, so just forget the idea, see?"

"Yes, I will," she said helplessly.

Fay was out and they were just finishing lunch. Hilary drew a deep breath. "Dan

— I'm worried about Fay."

"Are you?" He went on eating unconcernedly. "Why?"

"She . . . she seems so on edge."

He looked up and his eyes were shrewd. "You've noticed that?"

"Yes and . . . Dan, does she really believe in all that nonsense about witch doctors?" The words came out in a rush.

He grinned. "A lot of otherwise normal people do, you know."

"But YOU don't?"

"Of course not — nor does Fay." He helped himself to another slice of bread. "She's just teasing you."

"Do you really think so?"

He smiled at her. "Yes, I do. Don't worry about Fay, Hilary, I'm keeping an eye on her so she'll be all right."

"But Dan . . . " Hilary took another deep breath. "She's so on edge. These — these phone calls that aren't . . . if you know what I mean."

He laughed outright. "Yes, I know what you mean. Don't take any notice of those either, Hilary. Some people have a perverted sense of humour and it's often

257

happened before — they think it's a joke to ring somebody up night after night so that they get worked up about it. Which is just what you are doing, isn't it?"

She felt herself relax. "You really think that is all it is?"

"Yes, so forget it."

But it was not as easy as that. For she had not told Dan everything. She felt guiltily that she should have told about Carlos, and the way Fay took Petrus and Carl to town and came back without them and then in a while there would be the telephone warning of *Fire*. She was afraid to tell Dan lest Fay be involved — but wasn't Fay already involved? And shouldn't Dan know so that he could do something to stop it? Yet what evidence had she? She could not prove that Fay was involved with Carlos, it would be Fay's word against hers. Nor would the fact that Fay's trips to town always coincided with the outbreaks of fire be called 'evidence' — it might just be chance.

One day there was another little episode that seriously alarmed Hilary — but, once again, it was not something she liked to tell Dan. Fay's explanation was, on the face of it, logical — though Hilary did not believe a word of it.

It happened on one of those afternoons which were becoming so frequent when Fay had taken Carl and Petrus into town and only Simon was left. Hilary had been sewing when she heard angry voices at the back of the house. She went outside and saw Simon threatening a very old African woman. Hilary recognised her as the old crone she had seen there before, bargaining with Fay. Now the old woman turned her head, saw Hilary, and hobbled forward, leaning on her long stick, mumbling through her toothless gums, her wrinkled face expectant. Simon tried to shoo her away; when that failed he got angry and grabbed her by the arm.

"Aiee . . . Aiee . . . " the old woman cried plaintively.

"Let her go, Simon," Hilary snapped. She did not like Simon; he had an arrogant, almost insolent manner and now he was staring at her strangely. "What does she want?"

Simon could speak English when he

wanted to. "The Madame," he said in a surly voice.

"Tell her the Madame is away."

"I have." He gave an expressive shrug and walked away, as if washing his hands of the whole affair.

The old witch-like crone hobbled nearer, peering into Hilary's face, holding out a package. It was an odd shape, wrapped round by a dirty piece of material. With an abrupt movement, she tucked the package under her arm and held up five fingers — three times. Then she fumbled in a fold in her grubby blanket and produced a shilling. And held up her fingers three times again.

It was easy to understand that she was asking for fifteen shillings for the package. Remembering when she had seen Fay talking to the old woman before, Hilary also remembered that Fay had held up her five fingers twice only. Well, maybe it was something Fay had ordered; maybe Fay would be angry if Hilary sent the old woman away. It was so difficult these days to do the right thing. Hilary went into the house and came back with ten shillings. She gave this to the old woman who recognised and accepted defeat graciously, grinning all over her face, grabbing the money, thrusting the parcel into Hilary's hands and hobbling away.

The grubby parcel had a very peculiar smell. Holding it between two fingers and as far as she could away from her, Hilary went to the 'clinic' but the rondavel door was locked. She hesitated, wondering what to do with it, not liking to take it indoors. Just then Samson came hurtling round the corner, bumping violently into her.

Totally unprepared for Samson's full weight hitting her, she was taken off balance, and the package fell out of her hand. As it dropped, the covering came off and something fell out.

Hilary stooped to pick it up.

On the ground lay a human hand. A dark chocolate brown hand, neatly severed at the wrist, caked blood congealed across it. The fingers were oddly long and curled, the palm of the hand a palish pink.

She straightened, still staring at it.

A dreadful nausea rose in her throat.

Samson was leaping about — in a moment, he might grab it. Somehow she found courage and took the cloth, hurriedly scooping up the hand, bundling the cloth round it and putting it on top of a tall tub that stood near the kitchen door.

Then she ran to the bathroom and was violently sick.

When Fay returned, she told her about it. "Why on earth did she bring you a human hand?" Hilary asked.

Fay was white with anger. "She could have come back another day."

Hilary stared at her in dismay. "You knew it was coming . . . What do you want with a hand . . . "

"I didn't want a *hand*," Fay said irritably. "If Simon wanted to get rid of her you should have let him."

"But I knew you knew her. I saw her here once before."

"I wish you'd mind your own business," Fay snapped. "I'm getting so tired of your perpetual snooping."

Hilary's cheeks were flushed. "Next time anyone comes with a parcel for you, I'll ignore it." She turned away

262

wearily, worried, alarmed, bewildered.

Fay's mood changed at once. She was contrite. "I'm sorry, darling, that I blew up. It's just . . . " she shrugged. "But really the whole thing is too absurd. I ordered some rather unusual bead necklaces. They're cheap and completely African and I find they make attractive presents. I gave her an order."

"But why did she bring that . . . " Hilary shuddered again.

"I'll ask Simon," Fay said. She returned in a while, looking very amused. "What a mix-up and a waste of ten bob!" She began to laugh. "Do you know what it was all about? It seems a *boy* who lives in her kraal got involved in a fight and his hand got cut off — she came to ask me to go with her to sew on the hand so that he might be well again," Fay chuckled. "What it is to have a reputation as a medicine man. I'm sorry you got such a fright."

"But . . . " Hilary began and stopped. What was the good? She managed to smile. "I'm getting used to frights in this country," she said mildly.

Even as she spoke, the telephone bell

rang sharply. Hilary went to answer it, knowing in advance what it would be. And it was. There was a general warning of fire, over in the direction of Solomon's Peak.

She went back and told Fay who looked suitably surprised. Hilary's heart was aching and she longed to ask Fay frankly if there was any connexion between her visits to Monsimbe and the fires.

"You didn't bring the *boys* home?"

Fay looked at her sharply. "The silly coons always keep me waiting and I get fed up with it. I've just sent Simon in for them."

— The fire is at Solomon's Peak. Why is it called that?"

Fay yawned. "Seems there is a legend that there was a certain African prince who used the peak for getting rid of refractory wives. They used to toss 'em over. Not a bad death really. A drop of something like two thousand feet, so it would be a quick end."

"Fay don't," Hilary said, shivering.

Fay looked at her. "We all have to die sometime. I'd rather die that way than slowly, wouldn't you?"

Hilary shivered again. "Don't let's talk of death. That hand . . . "

"Oh, forget it, and for goodness sake, don't mention it to Dan. He hates me running the clinic, says I'll pick up some obscure tropical disease one of these days."

"I won't mention it," Hilary promised.

* * *

It was a few days later that Philip came to the house. Fay had gone out to play bridge and Hilary was alone. She had been lying on her bed, having a siesta, when she heard the sound of a Rover. Thinking it might be Anna, who had half-promised to come to tea, Hilary hurried outside, hardly bothering to stop to comb her hair, looking flushed and rumpled.

She had a shock when she saw that it was Philip and that he was walking into the house with a very determined air.

"Fay is out — " she told him breathlessly.

He looked at her gravely. "I know.

That's why I came. I want to talk to you alone."

She backed before him into the sitting-room, nervous and not sure of what he wanted. This was the first time she had been alone with him since she heard him telling Fay he loved her. Now she looked at him curiously. Was he so very unhappy? He must be, if he loved Fay and thought it hopeless.

"You're not very hospitable," Philip teased. "What about some tea? Or are the *boys* out?"

They were. Once again, they had gone to Monsimbe with Fay. She was terrified that one day someone would connect Fay's trips with the *boys* and the outbreak of the fires.

"I'll see . . . " she said and escaped to the kitchen. Luckily the fire was alight though dull; she raked it, hastily stuck in some dry wood, pushed the kettle over the flames and prepared a tray. Then she went back to the sitting-room, feeling absurdly like a condemned man.

Philip wondered why she was looking so scared and he felt more troubled than before. She had changed so tremendously since her arrival in Africa. Her face had always been pale with that odd three-cornered look, but now the skin was drawn taut over the high cheekbones. Her mouth, once so young and happy, was now disciplined too much. Her friendly eyes were guarded. She was looking at him now, tense, automatically on the defensive. Why?

"How well do you know Carlos Antunes?" he asked abruptly, deliberately startling her for he wanted to shock a truthful answer out of her, for once.

She stared at him, her eyes dilated. "I . . . " Her cheeks coloured guiltily, "I don't know him at all." She jumped to her feet. "The kettle must be boiling."

She escaped to the kitchen. It had been the last question in the world she had expected.

When she did come back with the tray, Philip was standing by the open door, gazing at the distant plain. The azure blue sky was spattered with tiny white cirrus clouds, there was faint haze on the ground. He swung round, watching her put the tray down, pour out the tea, her shaking hands fumbling as he stared at her white frightened face. What lies was she inventing?

"How — how is Jackie?" Hilary asked, as she gave him his cup. "Tallulah told me that he had got over the bilharzia but that there were complications."

"Yes, but those are being smoothed out. I believe they've been advised to leave the district."

"Poor Jock," Hilary said, sipping her tea and nearly crying out, for it was very hot and burned her mouth. "It'll break his heart to give up his job."

"It would break Nancy's heart if anything happened to Jackie," Philip said drily. He abruptly switched the conversation. "You haven't answered my question." His voice was stern. "How well do you know Carlos Antunes?"

She stared at him miserably. "I don't know him at all."

"But that's absurd," he said impatiently. "You can't expect to get away with that. You can't deny that you met Carlos in Monsimbe and introduced him to Mrs. Adams and several others."

She clenched her hands; what was she to say? To tell him that it had been a plot, contrived cleverly by Fay and Carlos? Would he believe her? And if he believed her, would it hurt Fay?

"Yes, I introduced him but . . . "

"And you said that you met him on the plane," Philip pursued ruthlessly. "Didn't you?"

There was a lump in her throat, so she just nodded.

Philip sat down, straddling a chair, leaning on the back, his lean face stern. "Now why did you tell such an outrageous lie?"

There was silence. Philip went on. "Such a stupid lie. But then all your lies are stupid."

Hilary's head jerked up — her mouth opened, and closed again. He waited. When she did not answer, he continued, his voice contemptuous.

"Your lies can always be found out. You should be more careful what you say. I was on the same plane coming out from England and that man was not on board." Silence, again. He leaned forward. "Was he?" he snapped.

"No."

He relaxed. "Well, that's one admission.

How did you meet him, then?"

She looked away from him, looked round the room, but there was no escape. Should she tell the truth? Say that he had come here to see Fay?

She tried anger as a defence. "Why do you want to know? What business is it of yours?"

"It is my business," he said coldly. "I have every reason to believe that this man is at the back of the poaching campaign, and I mean to get hold of him."

Hilary's whole body seemed to shudder. She tried to speak, swallowed, tried again. Fay was mixed up with the poaching. It all added up. Carlos must have some hold on her — that was why Fay was so afraid, even though she tried to brazen it out. So that when there was a fire, there was always some poaching done in a different neighbourhood, as Dan had told her. Was that why Fay always took the *boys* to town? Did they — or Fay — start the fires?

She looked at Philip's watching face and was suddenly convinced that if she told him the whole truth he would understand — his love for Fay would help him find a way to get the whole business cleared up without involving her.

"Philip . . . " she began. She would tell him everything — even about the human hand.

But Philip did not hear her. His patience, already stretched to breaking point, snapped. He stood up. "I'm sick and tired of your senseless lying," he said crossly. "Where's the point in it? Somehow or other you've got mixed up with this man. Don't tell me you're in love with him." He sounded disgusted. "Even if you were hurt badly in England, there's no need to go about making a complete fool of yourself. Falling in love with Dan — and then with Jock — and now with this man."

The words had died on Hilary's tongue. She stared at him, horrified.

"What do you mean?" she said stiffly. "I was badly hurt in England?"

He turned away with a quick, irritable movement. "I shouldn't have let you know that Fenella — I mean, Fay — told me about it. I know it must have been humiliating to get to the church to

271

be married and find the man hadn't turned up — " he ignored her horrified gasp. "Fenella — I mean, Fay — told me that was why you invented those silly lies about her child and that she needed you. I can sympathize, in a way, but I think you're behaving extremely childishly. Falling in love with every man you meet, making a fool of yourself."

She was on her feet now, holding the back of the chair, shaking all over. So Fay had told all those lies about her — and goodness alone knew how many other lies. And he believed them. He believed she could be as silly as all that.

He stared at her. How pale she was — how young — how very vulnerable. He had an overwhelming desire to take her in his arms and comfort her. And yet her very stupidity made him angry. Women! Once they entered your life, trouble began. Look at Fenella and the endless scenes there had been. When Fenella loved, she loved to extremes, he thought ruefully. There had been so little between them but to Fenella, it was the greatest tragedy that they must part.

He thought back to the first time

he had seen her, standing out head and shoulders above the rest of the crowd because her personality was like a blazing banner. Their eyes had met. He had avoided as long as he could but within an hour, she had been at his side, holding her glass towards him. "Be a poppet," she said, "and get me another drink." And when he obeyed and returned, she had introduced herself, her eyes wide and appraising. He had been amused by her frank approach. Fenella had no inhibitions — when she wanted a thing, she went after it. Sometimes her ruthlessness shocked him, yet he could understand it. He thought it the greatest pity she had married Dan — they were neither of them right for each other. Fenella needed life in a big city, married to an important man where her gift for making friends would help him. Here in this small community where friendships flared so easily into flirtations and, if you were not careful, into something more — and where tongues wagged because there was nothing else to do, what could have been an asset to a husband, was a liability.

It had been at their third meeting that he knew he was in love with her. They had been talking quite casually, and without rhyme or reason both had fallen silent, looking at one another. Then both had spoken at once, saying each other's names. They had both known what was happening. He had called her Fenella because, right from the beginning, she had told him how she hated the name Fay and loathed even more, Dan's ugly nickname of Effie; that she always wished to be called Fenella. So it had become his name for her. He had not liked finding himself in love with a married woman, especially when she was his friend's wife, so he had gone to England to try to get the whole affair in the right perspective, had met Hilary on the way back, then seen Fenella and realized that it was no longer the urgent painful emotion it had been. But it still was for Fenella. He had tried to avoid her but whenever he went to Monsimbe, Fenella was there. She even went to his house — she worried him to death. He had begged her to be cautious; they did not want any talk. And then she had asked him to come to her home to see her; he had agreed, hoping it would end the affair.

But the farewell interview had gone wrong, somewhere. She had wept, had said he was killing her, that he no longer loved her. He said he did love her — which was true, but not in the way she meant, or in the way he had loved her originally. He still loved her gaiety, her impudence, her voice, the way she smiled, the way she looked; but it was more affection than love, for he was sorry for her. He felt she had been too young when she married, that she had married as an escape — never a good reason — and that she was a very disappointed woman.

"But if you love me," Fenella had said, "you would want to marry me."

He had tried to show her why they must be sensible and part. His religion was against divorce, he said — which was true. He loathed divorce — and all the consequent reactions. He had seen too many of them. "And I think the meanest thing a man can do is to steal his best friend's wife," he had added. It sounded priggish but it was also the truth.

She had put her arms round him, her cheek against his. The tantalizing fragrance from her hair left him cold. He had thought sadly that nothing was so dead as a love affair that is over. Not that theirs could be called a 'love affair' — he had kissed her half-a-dozen times, not more. Snatched, exciting, meaningless kisses, made sordid by fear of being seen.

"If I was free, would you marry me? I mean — if Dan died?"

He had felt safe, coward that he was, and unwilling to hurt her. "Dan is young and healthy — don't let's build castles in the air."

She had refused to laugh, had looked at him gravely. "He takes risks when he's on safari — supposing he got killed, then I would be free."

He had laughed again. "A crack shot like Dan get killed? Not likely."

She had persisted. In the end, he had lied, had said he would marry her if she was free. And she had seemed content. Somehow that made him feel worse. His only comfort was that if a new man turned up, she would transfer her affections. Poor darling Fenella, with her romantic heart and her habit of dramatizing the least likely of situations, how he wished he could think of some way of helping her to happiness.

He was suddenly aware that Hilary was still staring at him, her eyes full of tears. He acted without thought, going towards her, taking her in his arms.

"Darling — " he said, "Don't look like that. Life isn't over because some damn fool of a man didn't recognize his good luck in winning you . . . " He felt her relax for a moment, then felt the slight body resist him. His arms fell away and he looked up; standing in the doorway, smiling at them both, was Fenella.

"Well, well; it's Philip now, is it, Hilary?" Fenella said in honey-sweet tones. "Having exhausted the man-power here, you're reduced to him."

Hilary turned to stare at her — her face quivered, her mouth trembled, she turned and ran, slamming the two doors between the lounge and her bedroom.

There was a silence and Fenella walked into the room. Philip said quickly:

"I didn't hear the car."

"Obviously." Fenella looked at him, lighting a cigarette with hasty, jerky movements. "Obviously. So you and Hilary were having a nice little love scene, eh? Well, well, wonders will never cease."

"You're quite wrong," he said firmly. "I came here to ask her what she knew about Carlos Antunes?"

Fenella looked at him, her thin brows arched. "And did she tell you?"

"No, damn it, she didn't. What do you know about him, Fenella?"

She shrugged. "Just that Hilary's scared to death of the man."

"I've got someone checking on him," Philip said, turning to the door.

"Good idea," she said calmly. "It worries me to think of a kid like Hilary mixed up with him." She walked with him to the Rover, leaning against it, smiling in at him. "Everything organized for Hilary's safari?"

"Yes — we go on the tenth. Okay?"

She smiled. "Okay. I'm looking forward to it. We might even have the chance to be alone for a few moments, darling . . ." Her hand brushed his cheek gently.

He felt uncomfortable. "Please — Fenella — we said — "

She watched the Rover go down the hill and then went back into the quiet house. At any moment now, the telephone would ring and down the party line would come the dreaded word FIRE . . . and Philip, Dan and the others would go racing off — while fifty miles away, Carlos and his men . . .

She smiled and lighted a cigarette, looking into the empty grate, tapping her foot. She had received a nasty shock when she had seen Hilary in Philip's arms, but Philip had explained. All the same, Hilary was becoming a nuisance.

Fay began humming under her breath. Ah well, only four days to wait and then they would go on safari. And an awful lot of strange things could happen there. She turned to the bookcase and looked through the books, chose one and sat down, reading it, a smile on her mouth. It was a book of short stories by Ernest Hemingway.

14

THE tenth dawned bright and clear. Dan and the two girls drove down the hill and met Philip at the cross-roads. Hilary had purchased khaki shirt and trousers and strong, calf-high boots and looked just about as incongruous as she felt. She was very conscious of how Fay's clothes suited her, with her tall slim body, her incredibly long lovely legs, and of how funny she, herself, must look. They went in the station wagon with Philip, Fay automatically sitting in front while Hilary got in the back. Next followed Dan, driving the truck with all their gear, then another truck full of Africans. Dan had made Hilary laugh the night before when he had told her of some of the things they would take with them — paraffin refrigerator, oil stove for cooking, wash bowls on stands, a collapsible bath, fresh fruit, water filters, masses of tinned stuff. Fay had not laughed — she had said there was no sense in being uncomfortable unless you must.

Philip drove fast but somehow Hilary was not afraid. She sat, enclosed in her own thoughts, quite unaware that Fay was getting irritable because Philip kept looking back at Hilary. Hearing Fay's unconcerned laughter, she wondered at her.

She had asked Fay how she could tell such stories — such cruel unnecessary lies about her own sister.

Fay had laughed. "They weren't unnecessary, darling, on the contrary."

Hilary had stared at her. "But why? Why?" she kept saying.

Fay had shrugged. "Ask no questions and you'll be told no lies," she said flippantly, turning away. It was like banging your head against a brick wall but Hilary persisted.

"Carlos Antunes is obviously going to get caught — oh, Fay, I'm so worried about you."

That had really amused Fay. She had laughed loud and long. "Worry about yourself for a change. If Carlos gets caught — which is most unlikely

— you'll be involved."

"I shall tell Philip the truth." Hilary faced her.

Fay chuckled. "Try it and see what happens. He won't believe a word you say. He trusts me." She drew herself up, tilted her chin and smiled. She had walked out of the room.

They were driving a considerable distance to where the game was plentiful. The animals, Philip said, looked for water when there was drought. At the moment, there was a very bad drought in the neighbourhood, hence the shortage of game.

"Plus the poaching," Philip added grimly and glanced in the mirror to see what effect his words had on Hilary. But she was sitting stiffly, her eyes tightly shut, her mouth turned down at the corners. He wondered what she was worrying about now; how deeply involved she was with this Portuguese crook. The difficulty was to get evidence; to catch him red-handed.

The car was grinding down to cross the river which was a pebbly ford. He revved the engine as the car crawled up the steep opposite bank and they climbed a rise and went on through the crowded trees until suddenly they came to a huge grassy prairie-like opening. A herd of giraffe were grouped round a water-hole — they turned startled heads and began to lope off with their queer movements. Philip looked over his shoulder quickly. Hilary was still sitting stiffly, her hands folded in her lap like those of a well-behaved child. She was staring straight ahead as if uncaring, completely oblivious of the scene before them. How odd. Once she would have been crying out with excitement, craning her head, half-falling out of the car with eagerness.

They made camp that night close to a river. It was a narrow, very deep river, twisting and turning through tropical undergrowth, with here and there a bald-looking sandbank.

It was luxury with a vengeance, Hilary thought, and wondered what people in England would say if they saw how comfortable you could be on safari.

There was a double fly veranda tent where they sat with drinks. Two *boys* wearing long green cotton robes and white caps, moved about efficiently. Then they went into the dining tent where there was a complete mosquito netting so that the side of the tent could be rolled up and it was just as if they were in the open air and yet without the mosquitos plaguing them. They could hear the hum of the mosquitos, hear the slight crash as a moth banged in vain against the netting, attracted by the buzzing flaring light of the pressure lamps.

It was an extraordinarily good dinner of tinned chicken and vegetables, followed by tinned fruit and thick cream, and strong Turkish coffee.

"You do yourself well, Philip," Fay said softly.

Philip smiled, feeling acutely uncomfortable, wishing Fay would not look at him like that. Supposing Dan noticed.

"I hope you've got a generous licence and we can kill lots of game," Fay went on, holding out her glass for another liqueur.

"Yes, but this is Hilary's safari, don't forget," Philip said, in a rather forbidding voice. "What do you want us to hunt, Hilary?"

She had been thinking, her face quiet. It was an effort to come back to the bizarre scene, to focus her eyes on him.

"I don't want to kill anything."

"Well!" Fay exploded. "There's gratitude for you. Philip goes to all the trouble and expense of organizing this and you don't want to kill anything." She mimicked Hilary's voice.

Dan spoke quickly. "She's not the killer kind. I've brought a cine camera for you, Hilary. I thought we might arrange some good shots for that."

His was a friendly voice. Hilary smiled at him with gratitude. "That would be marvellous, Dan."

Fay lifted her eyebrows, looked significantly at Philip, and shrugged.

"What about some bridge . . . ?" she asked.

"I'm afraid I don't play," Hilary said unhappily. She began to feel she was being a kill-joy; yet surely Fay knew that she could not play? She had been promising to teach her for weeks.

"Do you do anything?" Fay asked

285

irritably and stood up. "What CAN we do? I know," she laughed. "Let's all get nicely tight."

Philip was frowning, looking worriedly at Hilary. Fay drew a deep breath and held herself very still. She wanted to leap at Hilary. Philip was here — what right had Hilary to do this 'lost little girl' act and attract his attention?

"I think an early night is indicated," Philip said stiffly. "We're to be up at dawn tomorrow."

In the tent, which Hilary was sharing with Fay, she hastily undressed and climbed into the low camp bed, adjusting the mosquito netting on its frame, hoping hard there were no ants or poisonous spiders in the bed. She lay with her eyes closed while Fay undressed. Neither girl spoke and the silence between them seemed to Hilary to crackle with hostility. Hilary found it hard to forgive Fay for telling Philip such lies about her and Fay now seemed to dislike her so much. One thing, as soon as they got home, she would be able to leave, Hilary thought. She would fly to Salisbury first, and see something of Rhodesia before deciding where to go next. Odd how terribly alone you could be; how terribly desolate you felt when there was no one to care about what happened to you. Her few letters from her father had shown her that he was very happy in America, that he felt — and his Bishop said — that he was doing a 'good job' and it might be a long time before he came home to England.

There were strange noises in the night. Hilary lay stiffly, aware that there were guards outside and yet still fearful. An awful cry set her trembling and wide awake again, and then she realized it was probably a hyena. A lion coughing far away, and in the background, suddenly, the dull throbbing of drums — a sound that in Africa goes on so interminably that, in the end, you almost cease to hear it. She lay wide awake, hearing Fay's tranquil breathing, convinced that she would never fall asleep.

But when she opened her eyes, the sun was just appearing and Fay was up, the camp in a bustle. Hilary hastily dressed, carefully shook out her boots to make sure there were no scorpions in them, went out to the portable wash basin and washed her face and cleaned her teeth, crouching before a small mirror to make-up her face. She found Dan in the dining tent, making some notes in a small book. He looked up and his eyes were friendly for a moment.

"Where's Fay?" Hilary asked as she sat down.

"She and Philip have gone off to reconnoitre," he said curtly. "We won't wait breakfast."

It came, almost at once. Fried kidneys, sausages and tomatoes and somewhat flabby, smoke-blackened toast. They ate in silence, Hilary afraid to look at him lest it start up questions. Did Dan know that Philip and Fay were in love? If he knew, surely he would not sit down quietly under it? Or perhaps he was waiting. Perhaps he knew that everything passed if you were patient — and he believed 'Effie' would soon grow tired of Philip.

"There they are — " she said impulsively as the station wagon came in sight. Fay and Philip walked across the stubbly

288

grass, two tall, very good-looking people. Their arms swung by their sides and Hilary had the feeling that, had they been alone, their hands would have been clasped.

Philip seemed ill-at-ease and very apologetic because they were late. Fay sat down and pulled off her shady hat. "I'm starving — hope you haven't eaten everything," she said.

That day they walked miles down narrow paths through the trees — the filtered sunlight green because of the interlaced branches overhead. It was scorchingly hot so that the least motion made the sweat run down their backs and their faces were beaded with it. From the trees hung ropes of greenery and every now and then, there would be a frenzied angry chattering and the monkeys would come swinging down these ropes from tree to tree. Hilary carried the cine camera and hoped she would remember all the things Dan had told her about it. Dan led the way in the procession with Fay next, then Philip, then Hilary, and behind her the African guards. All the men and Fay carried their guns at the ready — only Hilary was unarmed. Philip had given her a revolver — better than nothing, he had said — but he told her there was no need to worry, nothing ever went wrong on his safaris.

He gave a consoling friendly smile as he spoke but she stared at him blindly and he felt oddly rebuffed. If she didn't want his help . . . Hilary had not even seen the smile. Now she could hardly bear to look at Philip, knowing he believed her a liar.

She tried to take an interest in her surroundings. She might never have such a chance again. Hundreds of tiny, gaily-coloured birds were flitting through the trees; there were huge butterflies fluttering. Every now and then, they caught a glimpse of a buck or a herd of wildebeeste in the distance, for occasionally the closely packed trees would break up into open spaces. Huge trees could be seen uprooted — other trees leaning heavily against one another as if needing support. Dan had explained that there were often very bad storms and the lightning and tornado-like winds simply uprooted trees and flung them about.

They stopped for lunch under an aged baobab tree, and suddenly one of the African guards, a bow-legged little man with arms that were thin yet bulging with muscles, lifted his hand. All listened. At first Hilary could hear nothing, and then she caught the sound of the drums.

The bow-legged guard's face was stern. He listened and turned to Philip and spoke hastily. Philip looked grave, looked at Dan and both nodded.

"I'm afraid we'd better turn back," Philip said, studiously keeping his voice casual. "We'll find nothing this way. Maybe we'll have better luck tomorrow."

There was suddenly action as the *boys* got to work and cleared up. Once again the procession set out — but first, Fay had a chance to speak to Hilary.

"Poor Philip is flapping like a mad thing," she said laughing. "He's terrified you'll get hurt."

"Me?" Hilary gasped. "But . . . but why ME?"

"Because you might lose your head

and that would be fatal," Fay said and turned away.

"But what's happened? Why are we going back?" Hilary caught her arm to hold her.

Fay smiled. "Because there are wounded leopards about. Wounded leopards are dangerous beasts, in case you don't know." She shook her arm free and hurried on, to take up her place in the procession behind Philip. He said something and rearranged the formation so that now Hilary had to walk between Dan and Philip.

They walked fast and in silence, the heat so unbearable that the sweat ran into Hilary's eyes and she kept stumbling. She felt Philip's hand on her elbow and she walked on, shaking herself free, determined she would not give Fay the chance to laugh at her.

They had not gone far when they heard a terrible crying. It sounded like a baby. The crying grew greater and more agonizing until they reached a clearing. There, on the ground, lay a small baboon, his body badly ripped, his voice raised in pitiful pleading. His whole stomach seemed to be hanging out of the torn body and his little hands were patting it as a baby might pat an aching tummy.

"Don't look, Hilary," Philip said sternly, swinging her round. She stood still, pressing her hands to her eyes, fighting nausea. There was a sharp crack of a shot and then Dan was by her side, his arm round her.

"It's all right now, Hilary." His voice was reassuring. "The poor little basket is out of his misery."

She leaned against him, still trembling.

"Nature in the raw is never pretty," Fay said lightly. "You'll have to learn to stomach these things."

The word sent Hilary off again, and she was violently sick. Dan opened a flask of brandy and made her drink a little. It burned her throat but it warmed her and stopped the trembling.

"What — how . . . ?"

"A wounded leopard — must have heard us and taken fright," Philip said curtly. "I suppose the whole tribe of baboons made off — but the mother might come back and then the situation could be ugly. If you feel you can, we should push on . . . "

"I'm ready," she said and wondered if she could walk a yard.

One of the guards said something — and everyone stood very still. Hilary could hear nothing but looking at Philip's face, she knew that he had. He spoke quietly and Fay and Hilary were put under a wide tree, while several of the guards stood round, their guns ready, the safety catches off. Philip and Dan and three other guards walked down the path slowly — and a sign made them glance slowly up. Hilary, watching them, also looked up and her heart seemed to stand still.

Crouched on a low branch of a tree, his body close to the wood, was a leopard. A long, vicious-looking animal, his mouth curled back, his whole body tensed to jump —

And he was looking at Dan.

Very, very slowly Dan lifted his Mauser . . .

In the same moment, Fay cried out. A smothered frightened cry. Dan half-turned and Hilary saw that Fay was levelling her gun, aiming. Suddenly — horrifyingly, Hilary understood everything. Fay was going to kill Dan.

Instantly, Hilary lunged sideways, knocking Fay's arm.

Then things happened so swiftly that she could never sort them out.

There was the crack of the shot, the snarl of the leopard as he sprang and the sound of another shot; and then everything was still.

And they were all running, to where Dan lay, his shirt ripped off him, his shoulder scarred with deep bloody wounds. Philip was on his knees, he looked up.

"It's all right, Fenella," he said. "He's not dead . . . "

Fay began to laugh — it was pure hysteria. Laughter and tears. Philip looked at Hilary. "Slap her face — hard," he snapped.

Hilary turned and obeyed. It was a hard slap, for Fay's frenzied sobs had seemed the last straw to a nightmare situation.

Fay stopped crying abruptly. Philip was issuing sharp orders. Several of the

Africans set off down the path, running lightly. Philip explained as he ripped off his own shirt and began to make pads to stop the bleeding. "I've sent them to the camp for a stretcher. We'll have to get Dan out of here and to a hospital as fast as can be." He spoke over his shoulder as he worked.

"Can I do anything?" Hilary asked.

"Haven't you done enough?" Fay asked bitterly. "If you hadn't lost your head and knocked my arm, I'd have shot that leopard and Dan would have been all right."

Hilary stared at her — opened her mouth and closed it again.

Philip turned his head. "What made you cry out, Hilary? Scared?"

"I didn't cry out," Hilary said. "It was Fay."

Fay looked shocked. "Oh, Hilary, you can't expect us to believe that. Why, the very idea is ridiculous."

And Philip was looking at Hilary as if he despised her.

"We ought never to have brought you with us," Fay went on. "You're just a liability and now look what has happened. Dan will die . . . "

"I don't think so," Philip said.

"He will," Fay said very quietly and the tears streamed down her cheeks.

Dan stirred, so Philip dropped to his knees. He looked up, puzzled.

"His back — he's complaining about his back." He looked at the improvised bandages he had wrapped round Dan's shoulder and body. "I don't like to take them off for the bleeding might start again."

"I think he's shot in the back," Hilary said quietly.

Fay rounded on her. "Do shut up, Hilary. I can't stand it. Who shot him in the back?"

Hilary looked at her, at the tear-filled eyes, the distorted face. "You did."

Philip stood up, and took her arm. "Look, Hilary," he said coldly. "I don't know what your game is but please pipe down. I've enough trouble on my hands without having you make Fenella hysterical. We'll just have to wait. We'll argue about it after Dan is safe in hospital."

It seemed an endless wait — with Dan

lying so still, his tanned face getting whiter, his mouth a pinched line. Philip and Fay smoked ceaselessly. Hilary just stood and stared ahead. It was a relief when the African *boys* arrived, carrying an improvised stretcher made from a camp bed.

It was a slow agonizing journey back to camp, with the need to be constantly on the alert. Hilary was a little lightheaded by the time they saw the tents and when Philip told her curtly to get into the station wagon by the stretcher's side and gave her some brandy which she was to give Dan if he awoke, she obeyed silently.

Fay was to stay behind with the *boys* to see the camp packed up and to drive the truck. She looked at Hilary with angry eyes. "If you knew how to handle the *boys*, I could go with Dan."

Hilary sat very still in the jerking station wagon, watching Dan anxiously. Now and then, he would groan. He did not open his eyes once.

They had to drive very slowly because of Dan. Neither Philip or Hilary spoke. He was retracing the whole of the misadventure, step by step, trying to understand how Hilary could have lost her head and caused Fenella — a crack shot — to miss the leopard. The animal had been a perfect target, crouched on the branch of the tree. And how could Hilary turn round and accuse her sister of shooting Dan? It didn't make sense. He was filled with a sense of urgency, desperately worried about the leopard's claw wounds on Dan's shoulder lest sepsis set in.

Hilary watched Dan's white face and wondered if Fay was right and Dan would die. Some of the shock was wearing off now and she could begin to think. And the more she thought, the more she grew afraid.

Fay was mad. That was the obvious solution of everything. Of Fay's 'amorality', of her association with Carlos, her belief in witch doctors, the Africans' fear of her. It all added up. And her 'heart's desire' must have been the death of Dan . . . and the witch doctor's idle words must have given her the idea.

But what now?

Hilary twisted uneasily as she squatted

by Dan's side. What would Fay's next move be? There was only one person who could testify against Fay — could say that she had seen her aiming at Dan, and that was herself. It seemed incredible — utterly and terribly incredible that Fay could want to kill Dan. But if she was mad she could not be held responsible. And if she was mad enough to kill her own husband, what was to stop her from killing her own sister?

The station wagon jolted over a rock and Dan groaned. Philip looked back.

"Conscious?" he said curtly.

"No."

They drove on, still in silence. Hilary's mind whirled round and round like a frightened rat in a trap. What could she do? Would Philip believe her? Yet could she calmly sit back and let Fay murder her? Would Fay dare? But why not? Fay had the self-confidence born of madness — she would believe herself too clever to be caught. And it could easily be arranged. Hilary's death could be made to look like suicide, and the reason given that Hilary felt herself responsible for Dan's wounds.

"Philip," she said out of her dry throat desperately. "Fay — do you realize that Fay is mad?"

"I think *you're* mad," he said angrily. "What is wrong with you, Hilary? You seemed such a nice girl — unaffected, genuine, and you've turned out to be rotten. Rotten right through to the core." He spoke bitterly, cruelly. He still could not understand the metamorphosis. How could Hilary have turned out to be so completely different from what he had believed? He knew that he had fallen in love with her — she had been so refreshingly different from most girls — and had even thought of marriage. But now — a liar, a cheat, a girl who deliberately tried to make her sister appear to be a would-be murderess and who was now trying to make out she was insane into the bargain.

"Philip," Hilary said, even more desperately, "you must believe me. It's Fay who has told all the lies. Mother and I honestly believed she had had Jackie, that there was a baby on the way. I was never engaged to anyone in England — Fay lied about that. That day the rogue elephant was shot, she took me to a witch doctor, he said she would get her heart's desire and she was very excited. Today — today when I saw her aiming at Dan, I knew she wanted to kill him."

He tightened his mouth. "Why should she want to kill him?"

"Oh, Philip, do you think I don't know?" Hilary asked bitterly. A terrible lassitude seized her. It was no good. He would not believe her. No one would. Fay was too clever. "I know that you and Fay are in love."

Before he could answer, there was an imperative toot of a horn behind them. He saw that Fenella had caught up with them and was now signalling them to stop. He knew he had been driving slowly but she must have driven at a crazy speed in that heavy over-laden truck. He drew over and let her pass and then stopped his station wagon as she stopped the truck a few yards ahead.

Fay came back, her eyes anxious. She looked sharply at Hilary and then at Philip. "How is he?" she asked the latter, pointedly ignoring her sister.

Philip took Dan's wrist in his. "I think

there's hope," he said reassuringly. "His pulse is surprisingly strong."

"I want Hilary to come with me," Fay said jerkily. "I can't bear to be alone. I'll take this truck to our house and then get the car. That'll get me to the hospital quicker, I'll be there nearly as soon as you are. Wait for me there, will you?"

Hilary opened her mouth. "I don't want . . . "

Philip looked at her, his eyes very cold. He opened the door. "Get out — " he said curtly.

It was difficult to move; she dragged her feet through the dusty road and climbed into the front of the truck beside Fay. Fay drove very fast, her face grim, saying not a word to Hilary.

The fear seemed to be piling up inside Hilary like a wild plunging thing . . . She looked back at the impassive black faces of the *boys* perched on the equipment and she knew she could not ask for help there.

When they were roaring up the hill towards the house, Fay said in a calm, conversational voice: "I could do with some tea, couldn't you?"

Hilary was so surprised that she could not answer. Had she imagined it all? For the first time she felt uncertain. How could she be sure that the gun *had* been aimed at Dan? Yet surely if Fay had been aiming at the leopard, the barrel would have slanted upwards towards the branch of the tree?

Fay stalked through the house, shouting for Petrus who came running from his room. Hilary sank into a chair, burying her face in her hands. She felt utterly exhausted.

Petrus came into the room with the tea, his bare pink-soled feet padding on the highly polished boards, his quiet deep voice greeting her politely. Fay came in and poured out the tea and passed Hilary a cup.

"Dan will die, you know," Fay said, still in a normal conversational voice.

Hilary looked at her and the homely familiar scene vanished and she saw that she was right. Fay was quite, quite mad. Her eyes were unnaturally bright, the pupils dilated. She kept mopping the corner of her mouth as though it were wet. Her hands moved the whole time, jerking at the tray cloth, straightening an ash tray, pulling a matchstick to pieces.

"Philip doesn't think so."

Fay smiled. "The witch doctor said so. That was why I was so excited."

Hilary felt sick inside her. "Did he — did he tell you to murder Dan?"

Fay went on smiling. "Not in so many words but he told me I would have an opportunity. And I would have had," her voice changed for a moment and became very cold, "but for you."

There was silence. Hilary thought wildly that if only she could keep Fay talking, Philip might come and rescue her. Not that he would come for that purpose, but he might leave Dan at hospital and grow tired of waiting for Fay and come here to see her.

"Fay — are you in love with Carlos?"

Fay laughed, shrill jagged laughter. "You little idiot, of course not. I'm in love with Philip, surely you knew that? And he loves me." She waved her tea cup about. "He will marry me when I am free. He said so."

"Oh, really?" Hilary tried to sound

surprised. "But . . . but what about Carlos?"

"Are you really interested in Carlos?" Fay sounded amused. "You always were a little nosey-parker, even as a kid. All right — if you want to know, there's no harm in telling you, now."

The last word was so frightening in its implications that Fay had been talking for a few moments before Hilary understood what she was saying. It was a fantastic story told under fantastic conditions. Sitting opposite your sister and knowing that she was mad — that you were postponing the moment when she tried to murder you. Behaving as if nothing unusual was happening, trying to find the right thing to say to keep her talking.

Carlos had sought out Fay, when he learned by chance of her amazing command of the local African dialects and of her influence over the Africans.

"They're scared of me — they call me the white witch doctor. Carlos and I have been working together for some time. He wanted the kind of *muti* that sells so easily to Africans, such as lion grease, elephants' hair, human nails. You can get good money for such things and I had an inexhaustible supply here. You can even get good money for human hands . . . " Fay smiled as Hilary shuddered. "Yes, I had ordered that hand, all right, it was just bad luck you seeing it. I had told the old woman that I wanted a hand and she produced it. Like me, most of them will do anything for money. The bones — human bones — make valuable *muti*, you know. I also got a few leopard skins for Carlos. That was when he decided to organize a large-scale poaching plan. I helped him there and it pays well."

Hilary found her voice. "You start the fires?"

Fay looked vaguely annoyed. "Were you smart enough to twig that? I thought . . . Yes, I would leave Petrus and Carl in town and then go off and start a fire. Easy enough with the long dry grass and brisk wind. Then I'd send Simon to fetch Carl and Petrus and we'd all have an alibi if necessary."

"I can't believe you could do things like that . . . " Hilary said slowly. "What would Dan say? Or Philip?"

Fay chuckled. "I knew I'd shock you. I

love the way your smug little face tightens up with disapproval. Dan would be mad as hell and Philip wouldn't believe it. I tell you, he loves me and I can do no wrong. Odd how different we are. I always hated you, you know," she went on, her voice still mild. "You were the parents' pet — you could do no wrong. Father used to rant and rave at me for hours and invariably he would end by asking me why I couldn't be like you." She laughed scornfully. "Even Mother didn't understand me — I think I frightened her, made her think of her brother . . . " she stopped abruptly, her teeth biting into her lower lip. "I've had more fun in my life than you'll ever know. Not that you'll get the chance," she said quietly. "You know that I'm going to kill you, don't you?"

Up until then, Hilary had clung to the idea that she might be wrong — that the whole thing was a nightmare and she would soon awaken. Her eyes flew to the telephone and Fay laughed.

"I cut that as soon as we got in. Do have another cup of tea. Your last."

Hilary passed her cup. She told herself

to remember what Dan had said — that Fay loved to tease. This was just a game . . .

"Fay — you won't be able to get away with it," she said desperately.

"Of course I will. I'm clever. Dan may recover but he'll never come out of that hospital alive. I'll see to that. I have a drug they can never trace — if he is having other drugs as well, as he will be. Then Philip and I will marry and we'll have his money and mine. We'll go round the world and . . . "

"If it's money you want, you can have mine," Hilary said huskily.

"No — it's not only your money," Fay said. Abruptly her face changed. She stood up, went to the desk and unlocked a drawer, drew out a cigarette. She lit it and stood for a few moments inhaling deeply. When she turned, her eyes were fixed and staring, her face rigidly set. "I want to get rid of you. Playing up to Philip — " she almost spat out the words. "He's mine — mine, I tell you. You know about Uncle Charles, don't you? He was the bogey Father held up before me whenever I wanted to have

309

any fun. Well, I am like Uncle Charles but I won't be caught. I'll have a perfect alibi — " she leaned forward, her eyes staring queerly into Hilary's face. "Uncle Charles was mad — mad as a hatter, and so am I. I've always been different from other people," she went on proudly. "It's all right to be mad if you're clever, and I am clever."

She turned and stalked out of the room. The silence was so startling that it was frightening. Hilary stood up, hardly able to move. She looked round wildly — was there nothing she could do?

And then Fay came back — Carl and Petrus behind her. Both *boys* had the same fixed staring look, both moved automatically. They were breathing fast.

"They will kill you," Fay said quietly. "And after they are gone, I will stab myself and be found, lying by your side, bleeding to death. But you will be quite dead."

"And Carl and Petrus — are they willing to hang for it?" Hilary gasped. She looked at the *boys* but they were moving towards her slowly, not hearing her words, almost as though hypnotized.

Fay laughed harshly, a terrible sound that rasped the quiet room.

"They won't remember a thing. I've drugged them." Fay waved her hand and said something Hilary could not understand.

Carl and Petrus moved forward, hands outstretched.

"Stop that," Hilary said sharply. "Don't touch me . . . "

She heard laughter and felt Fay's hands on her ankles, jerking up her legs. Her head hit the stone floor heavily — and everything went mercifully black.

15

WHEN Hilary opened her eyes, the bright glare of an overhead light made her close them again. She seemed to be floating in space but she felt a hand on her arm and then a slight prick and she knew no more. Several times she awoke and was aware of a dull ache in her head and an inability to move but finally she woke up and saw Philip sitting by her side and her head suddenly cleared.

He heard her make a sound and turned his head to look at her. She was shocked by his haggard face, the way his eyes were deeply set. Had he been ill?

He took her hand. "How do you feel?"

"I don't know — " she said honestly. And then she remembered and all the awful horror of those last moments when Fay had grabbed her ankles and helped her towards death, returned. It was all Philip could do to bear it as he saw the fear in her eyes. Would he ever be able to make her forget? Even as he looked at her, her face seemed to shrink away, her eyes grow larger and larger, still filled with fear.

"She was mad . . . " Hilary whispered. "She couldn't help it."

"I know." His voice shook. "I know. She's all right."

"You're sure? She isn't — hurt?"

"She's all right, my darling," he said, "I promise you."

He wondered at her surprised expression but then the nurse came hurrying, to give her an injection and sent him away.

The next time he saw Hilary, there was a little colour in her cheeks but her eyes were still shocked and afraid.

"What happened?" she asked and he knew she had to know. "Did you come back?"

"Yes," he said gently. "All the way to the hospital with Dan I remembered your face, the way you walked to the truck. I began to wonder . . . "

"But you didn't believe me."

"No, I didn't believe you," he said sadly. "I should have known better."

She touched his hand. "I don't blame you — "

"When I got Dan to the hospital they found a bullet in his back. I knew then that you had not lied — that she had been going to shoot Dan," he said unsteadily. "I can't begin to tell you how I felt. I had betrayed you — that sounds melodramatic but that's what it seemed like. I tried to phone . . . "

"She had cut the line."

"I got to the house just as . . . just as . . . "

"Fay grabbed my legs and tipped me up," she said lifelessly.

Philip looked at her worriedly. But the doctor had said that they must talk about it, that whatever had happened must come out into the open for if it was repressed it might affect Hilary's whole life.

"I was — just in time," he said, his mouth dry as he remembered the moment. The shrieking girl; the *boys* obviously drugged and ineffectual when Fenella ceased to issue commands; Hilary's terrible stillness.

"Fay?" she asked. He heard the

entreaty in her voice and knew that this was something else he must not shirk.

"She told me everything — about the *muti* and the poaching and . . . "

Hilary looked at him. "Where is she?" she closed her eyes for a second. "Philip, she was mad, quite, quite mad. Uncle Charles was like that — he murdered an old lady . . . Oh, Philip, have they locked her up?" Hilary's voice broke.

He held her hand very tightly. "No." Fay had not been mad but this was not the moment to tell Hilary that. That could come later. Fay had been temporarily insane but only as a result of taking drugs, a habit she had acquired. He could not understand why he had not guessed. Dan had, he had recently confessed. Dan had been trying to curtail her supplies but she had used the clinic as a blind for getting the *muti*. Dan had told him so much in the days while Hilary 'had lain unconscious, suffering from concussion. Dan was now up and about, slowly gaining strength but looking ten years older.

Hilary looked at Philip. "She's dead," she said in a lifeless voice.

He held her hand tightly. "It was better that way, Hilary," he pleaded.

She gave a little smile. "I know that. Much, much better. What — what did she do?"

"She threw herself off Solomon's Peak . . ." he began.

Hilary's face twitched and suddenly she was sobbing, great convulsive sobs that shook her body. He scooped her up in his arms as if she might have been a baby, rocking her, kissing her wet face, trying to soothe her. It was better for her to cry but it seemed to be tearing him apart.

At last she lay still. Completely relaxed, staring up at him.

"Are you very sad?" she said gently.

He looked down into her eyes. "I've so much to tell you, Hilary. I was in love with Fay — for a few months. I went to England to try to cure myself of it and met you. I came back cured, but Fay . . ." he hesitated and saw that she understood. "I still loved her for many things, her gaiety, her directness, her . . . her personality. What I can't understand, though, is how I could have doubted you. I loved you and yet I believed her."

"You love me?" she whispered.

"I won't rush you," he said quickly. "You've had a shock and . . . "

She smiled. "But I love you, Philip," she said honestly, "I always have. When I heard you tell Fay you loved her, I thought I would die."

He caught her close. "Oh, darling, can you ever forgive me?"

She put her arms round his neck and kissed him. "Philip can we live in your lovely house?"

"You don't mind staying here? You don't want to leave Africa — you won't hate it?"

"Of course not," she said, and the words came out in the well-remembered rush, "I love you and I love Africa."

He said something in an African dialect.

"What does that mean?" she asked curiously.

"I was quoting an African proverb which certainly applies to me. Translated, it means: 'MY HEAD WAS GREEN BUT NOW IT HAS RIPENED'."

THE WILDERNESS WALK
Sheila Bishop

Stifling unpleasant memories of a misbegotten romance in Cleave with Lord Francis Aubrey, Lavinia goes on holiday there with her sister. The two women are thrust into a romantic intrigue involving none other than Lord Francis.

THE RELUCTANT GUEST
Rosalind Brett

Ann Calvert went to spend a month on a South African farm with Theo Borland and his sister. They both proved to be different from her first idea of them, and there was Storr Peterson — the most disturbing man she had ever met.

ONE ENCHANTED SUMMER
Anne Tedlock Brooks

A tale of mystery and romance and a girl who found both during one enchanted summer.

CLOUD OVER MALVERTON
Nancy Buckingham

Dulcie soon realises that something is seriously wrong at Malverton, and when violence strikes she is horrified to find herself under suspicion of murder.

AFTER THOUGHTS
Max Bygraves

The Cockney entertainer tells stories of his East End childhood, of his RAF days, and his post-war showbusiness successes and friendships with fellow comedians.

MOONLIGHT
AND MARCH ROSES
D. Y. Cameron

Lynn's search to trace a missing girl takes her to Spain, where she meets Clive Hendon. While untangling the situation, she untangles her emotions and decides on her own future.

NURSE ALICE IN LOVE
Theresa Charles

Accepting the post of nurse to little Fernie Sherrod, Alice Everton could not guess at the romance, suspense and danger which lay ahead at the Sherrod's isolated estate.

POIROT INVESTIGATES
Agatha Christie

Two things bind these eleven stories together — the brilliance and uncanny skill of the diminutive Belgian detective, and the stupidity of his Watson-like partner, Captain Hastings.

LET LOOSE THE TIGERS
Josephine Cox

Queenie promised to find the long-lost son of the frail, elderly murderess, Hannah Jason. But her enquiries threatened to unlock the cage where crucial secrets had long been held captive.

THE TWILIGHT MAN
Frank Gruber

Jim Rand lives alone in the California desert awaiting death. Into his hermit existence comes a teenage girl who blows both his past and his brief future wide open.

DOG IN THE DARK
Gerald Hammond

Jim Cunningham breeds and trains gun dogs, and his antagonism towards the devotees of show spaniels earns him many enemies. So when one of them is found murdered, the police are on his doorstep within hours.

THE RED KNIGHT
Geoffrey Moxon

When he finds himself a pawn on the chessboard of international espionage with his family in constant danger, Guy Trent becomes embroiled in moves and countermoves which may mean life or death for Western scientists.

TIGER TIGER
Frank Ryan

A young man involved in drugs is found murdered. This is the first event which will draw Detective Inspector Sandy Woodings into a whirlpool of murder and deceit.

CAROLINE MINUSCULE
Andrew Taylor

Caroline Minuscule, a medieval script, is the first clue to the whereabouts of a cache of diamonds. The search becomes a deadly kind of fairy story in which several murders have an other-worldly quality.

LONG CHAIN OF DEATH
Sarah Wolf

During the Second World War four American teenagers from the same town join the Army together. Forty-two years later, the son of one of the soldiers realises that someone is systematically wiping out the families of the four men.

THE LISTERDALE MYSTERY
Agatha Christie

Twelve short stories ranging from the light-hearted to the macabre, diverse mysteries ingeniously and plausibly contrived and convincingly unravelled.

TO BE LOVED
Lynne Collins

Andrew married the woman he had always loved despite the knowledge that Sarah married him for reasons of her own. So much heartache could have been avoided if only he had known how vital it was to be loved.

ACCUSED NURSE
Jane Converse

Paula found herself accused of a crime which could cost her her job, her nurse's reputation, and even the man she loved, unless the truth came to light.

A GREAT DELIVERANCE
Elizabeth George

Into the web of old houses and secrets of Keldale Valley comes Scotland Yard Inspector Thomas Lynley and his assistant to solve a particularly savage murder.

'E' IS FOR EVIDENCE
Sue Grafton

Kinsey Millhone was bogged down on a warehouse fire claim. It came as something of a shock when she was accused of being on the take. She'd been set up. Now she had a new client — herself.

A FAMILY OUTING IN AFRICA
Charles Hampton and Janie Hampton

A tale of a young family's journey through Central Africa by bus, train, river boat, lorry, wooden bicycle and foot.

THE PLEASURES OF AGE
Robert Morley

The author, British stage and screen star, now eighty, is enjoying the pleasures of age. He has drawn on his experiences to write this witty, entertaining and informative book.

THE VINEGAR SEED
Maureen Peters

The first book in a trilogy which follows the exploits of two sisters who leave Ireland in 1861 to seek their fortune in England.

A VERY PAROCHIAL MURDER
John Wainwright

A mugging in the genteel seaside town turned to murder when the victim died. Then the body of a young tearaway is washed ashore and Detective Inspector Lyle is determined that a second killing will not go unpunished.

DEATH ON A HOT SUMMER NIGHT
Anne Infante

Micky Douglas is either accident-prone or someone is trying to kill him He finds himself caught in a desperate race to save his ex-wife and others from a ruthless gang.

HOLD DOWN A SHADOW
Geoffrey Jenkins

Maluti Rider, with the help of four of the world's most wanted men, is determined to destroy the Katse Dam and release a killer flood.

THAT NICE MISS SMITH
Nigel Morland

A reconstruction and reassessment of the trial in 1857 of Madeleine Smith, who was acquitted by a verdict of Not Proven of poisoning her lover, Emile L'Angelier.

SEASONS OF MY LIFE
Hannah Hauxwell
and Barry Cockcroft

The story of Hannah Hauxwell's struggle to survive on a desolate farm in the Yorkshire Dales with little money, no electricity and no running water.

TAKING OVER
Shirley Lowe and Angela Ince

A witty insight into what happens when women take over in the boardroom and their husbands take over chores, children and chickenpox.

AFTER MIDNIGHT STORIES,
The Fourth Book Of

A collection of sixteen of the best of today's ghost stories, all different in style and approach but all combining to give the reader that special midnight shiver.

DEATH TRAIN
Robert Byrne

The tale of a freight train out of control and leaking a paralytic nerve gas that turns America's West into a scene of chemical catastrophe in which whole towns are rendered helpless.

THE ADVENTURE
OF THE
CHRISTMAS PUDDING
Agatha Christie

In the introduction to this short story collection the author wrote "This book of Christmas fare may be described as 'The Chef's Selection'. I am the Chef!"

RETURN TO BALANDRA
Grace Driver

Returning to her Caribbean island home, Suzanne looks forward to being with her parents again, but most of all she longs to see Wim van Branden, a coffee planter she has known all her life.

SKINWALKERS
Tony Hillerman

The peace of the land between the sacred mountains is shattered by three murders. Is a 'skinwalker', one who has rejected the harmony of the Navajo way, the murderer?

A PARTICULAR PLACE
Mary Hocking

How is Michael Hoath, newly arrived vicar of St. Hilary's, to meet the demands of his flock and his strained marriage? Further complications follow when he falls hopelessly in love with a married parishioner.

A MATTER OF MISCHIEF
Evelyn Hood

A saga of the weaving folk in 18th century Scotland. Physician Gavin Knox was desperately seeking a cure for the pox that ravaged the slums of Glasgow and Paisley, but his adored wife, Margaret, stood in the way.